The Loss Of Some Detail

Mandi Martin

London | New York

For my mom and my brother, both a great support to me.
And to my Grandparents who have always been there for me.
Thank you for believing in me.

From the desk of: Silas Everett; Oculus mentis.

Forget all you know...for what you know may all be false...is the sky truly blue? Do our hearts really beat?

Perhaps existence is but a dream, a nightmare...maybe I am merely unhinged but what is sane and what is normal?

Madness to one is normality to another...and no person should judge...so heed the following tale, should it ever be surfaced, with an open mind, for if it be closed then it surely has no function...

We are none of us perfect...and I myself do not wish to be...for what then would one strive for?

Still...I have rambled enough, and so, good reader, I wish thee well.

Both blessed and cursed

Silas Everett

The austere building was dark as it sat lost in the surrounding of a heavy forest, the branches and thorns keepings prying eyes away and making it impossible for any to flee. Even the light seemed afraid to penetrate into the barred windows.

How the ragged trees remained impervious to the howls of the wind and barrage of brine and rain no one knew.

Situated on a long-abandoned island out to sea, it had been isolated when the rocky crags threatened to fall as the waves crashed against them eroding them daily with the beat of their icy strikes.

No doubt in years to come the stone would fail and fall to form a grisly tomb beneath the ocean taking away anyone left to perish.

It had been the perfect place for the temple of the insane.

Known 'affectionately' to those beyond the sea and over the shore as Oculus Mentis; Mind's Eye...for it was the pupil in the great turbulence of the mysterious waters.

Inside the cold, grey walls it was just as gloomy shrouded in shadows and filled with an air of hopelessness for any who were condemned to remain.

For in the midst of the cold and confusion there was indeed life of sorts although to the many that resided within the ivy entwined walls the touch of the reaper would have been preferable.

The rare sight of a smile from within the barred doors was normally one of malice or if not rapidly removed by the swift 'correction' of one of the staff.

Eventually spirit died.

Chapter One

With the sound of his footfalls echoing against the stone behind him James Grey made his way down the corridor toward the isolation block.

In his mid-twenties he was one of younger of attendants of the male section, slender in frame with slightly unevenly trimmed blond hair, this however was done on purpose to allow the fringe to fall over his right eye concealing the fact one was green and the other brown.

He had found out well before working there that it was more prudent in life not to stand out too much, being where he was had only reinforced that belief more strongly. Any discrepancy in appearance or thought was never looked on kindly.

With a far more sympathetic manner James was widely distrusted and reviled by his colleagues, he had seen such illness in his neighbour when he lived at home and had witnessed that treated with a kind hand the man had fared far better.

Granted he had not been cured, the voices and occasional mania continued but they were manageable, he had caused no unmanageable issues.

He recalled the day when the man's wife had passed away, he had been taken away as no other family remained or if they did, they had no interest.

The next thing they heard was he was dead. Death by his own hand.

Although it was never confirmed rumour was rife that the body had been in a less than satisfactory condition.

There were two or three other attendants who did do an iota

more for their charges but it was risky, despite being termed imbeciles most were very astute and knew how to manipulate to gain advantage.

The rest of the staff mostly saw them as tools to obtaining a wage, and not a good one at that.

After fiddling about for some time to find the right key James unlocked the iron door to the stale-smelling corridor.

• • •

Most of the inmates in isolation were tethered for both their own and staff safety but it was still advised to use the hatch on the door and enter only if something needed adjusting.

Working his way down the barren passage nothing seemed out of order, making brief notes as he did so, the patients were mostly quiet, either restrained or sat uncomfortably in their own world. Each so different in their mood and emotions it was impossible for him to see them as anything but humans.

It was for him however an unusual evening.

James had walked these passages so often and yet everything felt as if he were seeing things for the first time, his body working as an automaton performing his duties, duties he done hundreds of times and yet sensing he had never.

'Tis but the atmosphere,' James thought, suppressing a shudder 'I have been here so long it affects one at times. I have heard others tell of similar.'

He believed he had anyway, that seemed to be something else he could not remember.

'Tiredness. The disturbance of sleep must have taken a toll also.'

He ventured down to his final room, one of the larger ones that was reserved for the more affluent patients or at least those who had people to pay for what they believed to be better keeping. It afforded some privilege in the keeping of belongings but treatment would remain the same.

Looking at the list the patient wasn't named, it gave only a gender and a smudged and unreadable date.

It wasn't that unusual, when left out the papers often got

4

damaged from the carelessness of others and the elements themselves.

James rolled his mismatched eyes and tucked it behind the rest of the papers; if he was able, he could jot down the details later.

He pushed open the hatch, grimacing at the high-pitched squeal that felt as if it would pierce his eardrums. He could not see whoever was incarcerated there but the water jug was empty which meant he had to go in and fetch it.

Reaching for his belt James sorted through the keys that hung from it and pressed the correct one nosily into the lock, the clattering of iron reverberating off the stone walls.

• • •

The saying 'money talks' was evident; the cell was far larger than those occupied by the ones who had little. Furnished well with a proper bed covered by homely blankets, no doubt sent from the family of who dwelt there.

However, the grey walls remained the same as did the barred window, the view blocked by the ivy growing outside giving the shadows free reign over everything.

Only thin streaks of ambient moonlight managing to traverse through.

The sense of another presence was evident as soon as James set foot in the room, the feeling of eyes watching every movement.

Turning around slowly his eyes fell towards a rosewood desk that had been moved into the corner, green eyes met his own.

James couldn't recall seeing this inmate before, a pale man with long, silver hair that fell well past his waist and yet his face betrayed no age, the skin blighted only by a ragged scar across the right cheek.

The clothing worn was simple but well made, the white of the blouse appearing as if it were brand new, not a mark to be seen.

He sat cross-legged gazing evenly with a small smile tugging at his lips, tapping a blunted pencil on his thigh.

"Good morrow, Mr Grey..." He spoke in a pleasant drawl, a

clipped edge indicating good birth. "Always a pleasure to see a familiar face."

James blinked at the use of his name, wracking his brain to try and recall the man before him but drew a blank.

"It's evening," he replied simply and reached for the jug. "I only do night shifts."

"Really. Well it is hard to tell," the man said, his eyes never leaving him. "Day and night merge into one."

James made a sound of agreement before speaking again

"You will forgive me but do I know you?"

"Of course you know me!" The other seemed mildly insulted. "God knows I been here long enough!"

He exhaled in frustration and leant on the desk, placing the pencil carefully to one side before extending a hand as one did for a suitor, his fingers long and ending in immaculately manicured nails, a rare sight even on the outside.

"Silas Everett at your service."

After some hesitation James inched forward to take hold of the proffered hand but as he grazed the fingertips it drew back as if burnt.

"Now we are acquainted...again," Silas examined his nails as if fearing they had been damaged "...James..."

He smiled when he noticed the bemused expression.

"Did I not say I knew you? I remember even if you do not."

Getting up he sidled past him to reseat himself on his bed, giving a shrug as he did so, it had been difficult to gauge his height from his sitting position but upon standing Silas was nearing six-foot-tall, his hair falling to the hips of his willowy frame.

"Only exercise I tend to get."

James nodded slowly, his nerves on high alert as the other moved past him with a grace that rivalled the finest dancer.

"You look no worse for it."

Rising an eyebrow Silas appeared vaguely amused.

"Even money cannot make the fare here palatable."

"You may think me foolish for asking," James said carefully, wondering if this was merely a ruse used by a clever inmate "but how exactly do I know you? I assume it is just in passing, I cannot imagine myself forgetting someone as...unique."

"Forgetful, aren't we?" Silas said with a shake of his head. "We know each other *far* better than that. Well we did."

"Well, if you will excuse me, I have to refill your water." He took up the jug. "I am sure I will see you again, Mr Everett."

"Come now that is hardly very amicable of you."

"I have other work to do..."

Silas frowned

"I know I am the last on your list, you have told me that before."

"Have I indeed?" James sighed as he sorted his keys with his free hand. "Then forgive me for not trusting you, Mr Everett, but I have been duped many times before."

He back stepped towards the doors, watching as Silas gave an exaggerated roll of his eyes.

"You wound me," he sighed "I have never 'duped' anyone...not to a dangerous degree."

James raised an eyebrow but did not respond. It was the best way with some inmates, ignore them and get on with the job at hand.

He slipped swiftly from the room and locked it firmly behind him.

• • •

The asylum water supply was a single well set in the centre of the courtyard.

At least that they used it for the patients, the staff used it only as a last resort, their own water supply brought from the mainland.

The water from the well was never the best and refilled by rain often carried an earthy taste.

After the heavy rains coupled by the spray from the sea the cobbled ground was as slippery as black ice.

Even in the nicer weather it was unpleasant, surrounded by the intimidating walls and the feeling of unseen eyes from the barred windows.

The ominous tension it exuded was almost tangible.

At night it was far worse and James had lost count of the times he had fallen. He had been fortunate that the worst he acquired was a few bruises and wet clothing.

It was damp now and James had to watch his step, a hard feat in the sparse light given by a clouded moon and dim glow from inside.

After what seemed like hours, his fingers going numb from the chill of both the air and the jug he was holding, he reached the well without incident.

Placing the jug down with a metallic ring echoing about the empty courtyard James reluctantly gripped the slimy, frayed rope to haul the bucket from the depths.

He hated this, the twisted hemp was coated with algae as he pulled it up further and smelt worse than when the mildew ate through the curtains in the staff area.

It always seemed to take hours but pulling any harder or faster might have spilt the contents of the bucket or broken the rope.

Finally, it came within reach and James carefully leant over to transplant the contents into the jug.

Letting go of the pail it fell back into the obsidian depths with a resounding splash and James wondered how the old wood never shattered.

Still, it didn't and that was that. It was hardly a miracle he was going to lose any sleep over. He lost enough over other things.

Picking up the jug he gingerly made his way back inside. These were the only occasions he was thankful the void inside.

• • •

Silas was lying down when James re-entered and, looking over, sat up slowly.

"Wonderful. You did not fall down the well, that would have been most unfortunate!"

James frowned and placed the jug down heavily.

"Not disappointed then?"

"Of course I'm not!" Silas flicked his hair back and looked fixatedly at him. "Who else would talk to me then? I should be left in an eternal torment of silence and four walls."

He sighed, rolling his green eyes in a dramatic fashion that suited a theatrical environment far more than the one he resided in.

"You know I am a very friendly person, but alas no one understands me!"

He flung his arms out and flopped back to the bed with a squeak of rusty springs, his lengthy hair falling about him as if he were draped in greying cobwebs.

James coughed as he tried to stifle the laugher that was rapidly rising within him like the stormy tide beyond the walls.

Silas lifted his head and raised an elegant eyebrow

"No one takes me seriously either it seems." However a light chuckle rumbled from his throat. "Although I am perfectly sane, for myself anyway, but anyone who errs from what is deemed to be the norm seems to be castigated."

He groaned

"Whipped off the street like a common mongrel, apparently a relative knew. They could have at least given their *victim* notice. Peril of being the working class…"

James smiled, the caution he normally employed slackening somewhat, Silas's quirky, somewhat flamboyant, personality was one that was easy to relax around.

"Yes, people are strange."

Silas gave a lengthy sigh and sat up, resting his head on his hand.

"Aye, and although you do not recall, our agreement on that subject was partially the reason we got on."

"…You are still a human being," James said cautiously, his voice dropping to a whisper, "yet I mean so offence when I say it is will be hard to find someone, besides myself, who takes you seriously considering the…" he paused, searching for the correct word "… *predicament* that led to you being here, whatever it may be."

"Well if you ever find out what that *predicament* is then kindly inform me," Silas grumbled "I have had that many diagnoses since I have been here that if I was not considered insane before then I most certainly am now."

Laughing James checked the lacklustre pocket watch attached securely to his uniform

"I am afraid I have to leave you, Mr Everett. I doubt anyone would notice but I shall be in trouble if they do."

"Yes, you have mentioned that before also," Silas replied, exhaling sharply as he idly twirled a lock of his hair "I do hope next time you visit you may be able to recall our past conversations… it would save me having to hear what has been spoken already. Although I fear I may have to repeat myself…"

"I can but try," James smiled. "I cannot guarantee it though."

He was, quite frankly, still steadfast in the belief that this was still some ruse on Silas's part for his memory was normally faultless.

"So I am being hopelessly optimistic that we shall be back on first name terms then?"

Silas said with a woebegone expression.

"I am afraid so. But considering you seem to call me by mine anyway I have my doubts things will be that different."

James gave a polite nod in his direction, opening the door as wide as he dared before slipping through and sealing it securely behind him.

Chapter Two

James's room was nothing to write home about.

It had once been a storage room to house the various medications and other items of treatment until the lock had rusted in a copper dust and it had been too much effort to replace it.

Those whose job it was been to plan the layout of the building had overlooked the staff, apparently not thinking that they would remain there.

All things considered it was rather curious or rather stupid and because of this the bedroom space was scarce.

Due to the inhospitable location of the asylum and the reluctance of the boatmen to journey there it was only feasible to leave on the weekends and rather than dare the fickle tides a majority, most, if not all, of the staff remained on the premises, leaving only on special occasions. Meanwhile they utilised the upper areas as a makeshift dormitory and if the weather held fair they would take the rare day to venture to the mainland.

That is if they had anyone who wished to associate with them, the profession held a stigma that eventually those who guarded the insane would turn themselves.

James had no close family to speak of and had no reason to leave at all so requested to utilise the room as his own, at least it would be a private area for him alone.

Surprisingly the request had been granted.

Although when one considered his less than popular persona then it perhaps was not surprising at all.

But it was his.

And had space enough for the iron-frame bed and a small chest of drawers, not ideal for hanging his uniform up but if he folded it neatly then he could avoid too many creases. Pressing was not an option and sending it to the mainland, if they even did, was a hassle.

Flinging the heavy navy jacket onto the bed James closed the door with a sigh, his keys singing a discordant song as they clashed together.

He thought over the events of that day and how. Wait…what *had* happened that day?

James frowned, a sensation similar to a cramp gripping his stomach as he realised, he had no idea and a combination of panic and confusion embraced him.

Except for Silas he had no recollection at all. Much like the countless days before that.

'Tiredness…' James thought as he felt his head throb, aches rolling through his skull 'tiredness…'

He laid back on his bed, the lumps in the mattress oddly comforting, and stared at the yellowing ceiling and the crack that had started in the corner and had spread over the years. At least that was something he could remember.

It *was* a tiresome job and a lonely one, any talking between staff was kept to a few barely audible words, any louder and it would be resonated throughout the building and cause certain patients to react badly as well as annoy others on shift.

For the sake of placidness, it was worth keeping words brusque and brief.

James had another hour before he needed to do another check; with the inmates locked away he often spent the waiting time in the sanctity of his room.

In most institutes it would be against the rules, breaking it would be career suicide but out here rules seemed not to matter. Even if their handbook stated differently.

Had he not been on the nightly shift James had his doubts that he would have slept, the sounds seemed amplified in the dark, more despairing, more haunting.

Yet it was a benefit on this shift, when he was up here anyway, with the silence reigning he could sit peacefully but still hear if anything was going wrong.

He leant over to the nightstand to pull open the top drawer, rummaging under the socks and undergarments randomly thrown in.

Underneath there was a polished silver blade with an intricately carved handle, a forbidden item in any job but James knew he wasn't the only one to possess such things.

He wasn't sure why he had it, even where he had obtained it from, perhaps it had been a gift?

Whatever the reason it was there and it would feel strange if he was ever to look and find it missing. And concerning.

Fingering the handle he smiled to himself, the knowledge it was there gave both a sense of comfort and fear, an odd combination.

Placing his watch on the side James closed the drawer and lay back, he'd earned some relaxation if one could call it that.

But he did not dare close his eyes, sleep was hard to come by but he knew well that if he allowed them the luxury of closure they would remain shut and that was something he couldn't risk.

The sound of the soft ticking was almost soothing and for a while James forgot his confusion, allowing himself to relax and lose himself it those hypnotic notes to float in an aimless dream whilst still awake.

As happened every time as soon as he felt the least bit settled it was time again to get up…the minutes went by so slowly when he was tense.

Sitting up he pulled his jacket back on, fastening the bronze buttons neatly as he hoped the checks would be as smooth as they had been earlier.

• • •

As he ventured down the spiralling stairway James checked the ropes fastened across the precipice, it was a measure taken to prevent unfortunate 'accidents' if one of the patients managed to somehow get out.

Truthfully caging would have been a better option but the cost was high and keeping the inmate was too high a price in some people's eyes.

James could not actually see much point in the preventative measure, the upper floor was no longer used to house patients and the ropes would cause more damage than the plummet to the stone slabs below.

Pulling the crumpled list from his pocket he glanced at the names and the cell numbers, the ink was now smudged but still readable even though he should know all this by now, shouldn't he?

Probably. But he didn't and that was why it seemed strange.

The inmates all seemed placid as he once again echoed down the corridor, most sat on their beds, rocking like pendulums against the chill in the stagnant air.

Occasionally one would look up with empty, hopeless eyes before dropping them back to the floor to watch what no one else could see.

James felt a stab of sympathy as he watched them, marking the papers as he did so.

He stopped outside another iron door and flicked the hatch across; as he did so he heard the approaching sound of heavy boots on the concrete.

"Doctor..."

James nodded politely towards the grizzled man garbed in dirty white clothing, his chin speckled with stubble as if he had not shaved for several days.

His eyes were sharp and strained with, dark circles surrounded them yet they gave no discernible emotion.

"I would prefer it is you address me in the proper manner, Grey." The man's clipped voice was almost a hiss and James would not have been surprised to see a forked tongue slip from the dry lips. "So you will acknowledge me as Dr Morbridge or Sir...or not at all. I get enough lip from that effeminate creature you see to without staff adding more."

"Yes...Sir..."

It sounded better than speaking as if to a schoolmaster; James already felt like a chastised schoolboy and had no wish to feel even more like one.

Morbridge raised a cynical eyebrow.

"Better. Somewhat. Just get on with your job. However, I will let you know that I took patient twenty-three a while ago. He needed *extra* treatment."

Patient twenty-three.

James looked down at his paper. A man named T. Willis. He supposed it one less to worry about but the doctors tone made it hard not to.

He waited until Morbridge's footfalls faded before he continued himself, finding the doctor far more unnerving than the surroundings themselves. Unless they merely aggrandised his presence.

There was little to note as James continued his checks, the second and third never found much to do but as the night wore on often his job became more taxing.

Especially if some decided to become incontinent, an act that would certainly get the craved attention even if not the good sort.

His checks were swift, his last being the inmate he had conversed with earlier and a strange apprehension fell over him as he paused by the door.

Silas was lying on his bed tossing and catching a balled-up piece of paper repeatedly in consistent speed.

Even his blinks seemed to be timed to a perfect rhythm.

It was almost hypnotic to watch. Fascinating even, but it felt like watching a cobra sway and James did not want to be there for the strike, no matter how genial Silas seemed.

Backing away he carefully closed the hatch; if the other heard he gave no sign, never ceasing the constant toss and catch behind the iron.

Chapter Three

Apart from the normal hassles such as patients refusing to remain in their beds or purposefully soiling themselves instead of using the pot provided there was nothing unusual about James's shift.

But he wasn't disappointed when the clock finally read six and he was able to finish for the day, he needed sleep.

The morning sky was red through the trees as if the rising sun was weeping bloody tears, staining even the clouds.

The chinks of glowing light slipping through the boughs cast an eerie aura over the outside world, making the dew resemble rubies upon the fusion of green leaves.

Returning to his makeshift room James dropped face down onto his bed as he did there was a soft crackle from beneath the covers as if he had crushed a dead leaf.

Not bothering to even sit up James fumbled under the thin cover; his fingers clutched the creased surface of an envelope.

The white had yellowed as if it had lain there for some time and upon it was his name…nothing more, no address, no postage.

James let the letter drop onto the floor, he could read it later… his head felt full and ached from tiredness, whatever words were scripted within they would make no sense in his current state.

He drifted in and out of consciousness; one could not call it sleep, his mind too active and aware of the sounds and senses about him.

This continued until the late afternoon when his eyes would finally refuse to remain shut, the day to day noises didn't help.

The sounds echoed, banshee-like screams and clanging of the doors, a symphony of discordant music.

Sitting up James looked down at himself, his uniform was creased and his fingers still had the blackened stains from the lead of the pencil.

He felt too tired to have slept properly, having gone long past the stage where his mind could settle.

Getting up grudgingly he pulled out his spare uniform. He couldn't turn up like this, not even if his shift hadn't started.

The last thing he needed was more stress added to his collection.

It felt as if no time had passed at all, at least to his body, but the hands of the watch said differently and that was not to be disregarded as wrong.

Outside a few birds chirped amongst the greenery, their tunes muffled by the crush of leaves. It seemed they could sing even in Hell.

He cast another glance at the unopened letter, it would wait. Right now he, or at least his body, needed nutrition, if the food supplied even provided any.

Admittedly that which was served to the staff was far superior to that which the patients suffered. Some kind-hearted folk on the mainland would send donations of food and clothing but often the best was pilfered.

As were the items sent for those who lucky enough to have family members who still cared about them.

• • •

The dining area was large, and much like the rest of the building was devoid of any decoration or iota of colour to make it more bearable.

It was merely a vast stony room with two wooden table stretching long ways with matching, equally uncomfortable benches.

The barred windows allowed for little natural light enabling the shadows to reign and stretch their dark fingers over and above the filthy floors.

It did at least conceal a majority of what one was eating, not that it mattered when the repugnant concoction hit the palate.

James gave a polite but insincere greeting as he walked in, receiving a muttered reply from the handful of others there.

Their faces were so generic. Had he need to describe someone it would have been like describing a thousand of the same, but he knew them. He assumed he did anyway.

The nearest looked up as James moved passed him to his seat.

"Thought you'd moved to day shifts, Grey."

He spoke as if speaking through his nose or addressing an insect in a pile of manure.

"Obviously not," James replied in the same derisory tone. "I am unlikely to be turning out for extra work had I have been."

"The way you've been forgettin' things of late it wouldn't surprise me."

"Lack of proper sleep," James retorted, taking a chunk of bread from the plate on the table. "I find it rather awkward to get any."

His comment brought no sympathy or relation but nor did it bring any criticism since all present agreed that sleep was patchy at best.

The room became quiet again; the only sounds the standard noise of cutlery scraping and mugs being placed down.

"Can someone else check Nathaniel later?"

A white-haired attendant spoke up after a while, his face lined and sagging before his time.

"I twisted my knee seeing to one of those imbeciles and those damned stairs are hard enough at the best of times."

No one volunteered, their attention seeking anything other than the subject broached.

"I'll do it," James's voice seemed like thunder in a silent sky, "since most of you believe I don't pull my weight I may as well prove it."

The older attendant gave a snort of amusement; James hadn't dealt with Atrocity before.

When the man had been brought in no one knew his name and due to the gravity of brutality he had shown he had gained many appellations and none were overly complementary.

Even now they were not sure if Nathaniel was indeed what

he had been christened but it was the only one he had ever given himself and it had stuck.

"No argument from me lad," he said simply "but don't take it easy on him like you do with the rest of them, I guarantee he won't with you."

• • •

The worst affected patients were kept in the lower areas dubbed the tenth circle of Hell by some of the more learned staff.

There was no fire or fury but simply dank and darkness, the stench of mould lingering on cold walls where the fungus inhabited the cracks.

James, although educated, simply called it the basement.

The theory behind the design was simple; if one did happen to be astute enough to escape their cell then they would still have to navigate up the stairs and through the corridors to attempt to find as exit.

The chances of not encountering anyone along the way were almost impossible.

When one considered the location there was little need for the extra security except to make life more uncomfortable for those whose 'unsoundness of mind' had saved them a journey to the gallows.

There were only two down there so far, Nathaniel and another man who seemed to be completely placid, lost in a world of his own where no one else could find him.

Nathaniel however was in a different class.

In looks the paper had described him as 'one you would expect to see in the evenings as backstreet pimp'.

A bestial man he was powerfully built with dark blond locks and cruel eyes that saw past the skin and into the soul beneath. The feeling was so unnerving that the attendants had ordered him to be blindfolded even when alone in the room.

Strange patterns adorned his arms and back. Clearly done by another's hand and now covered in a thin black shirt, concealing the immoral markings from decent sight.

But it was his voice, a deep, throaty growl that chilled those who ventured in. The man seemed to know far more than he should.

Many a time a gag had been threatened but no one could get near enough, he had bitten a finger off someone in custody before and the images of the marks left upon the flesh of his victims were enough to keep from attempting it.

The corridor downstairs was far darker and the shadows seemed to dull even the echo of the feet that walked there.

James tried not to let it perturb him too much even though his mind kept surfacing quotes and passages of books. All relating to the dangers in the dark and what happens when one's voice doesn't echo.

The keys jangled as he shuffled through them; in the dark of the cell, empty save for a thin mattress, the other listened, deprived of much of his sight his other senses had been heightened.

A wolfish grin appeared; his teeth icy white in the gloom, and a soft chuckle emerged, unheard by the one outside.

As James entered, the shackled man stirred, his nostrils flaring to catch the scent of the one he lacked sight of.

"Fe fi fo fum, I smell the blood of an Englishman. His sister raped, his parent's dead, oh how he whimpered while they bled!"

James hesitated in the doorway at the sound of the mocking, sultry voice, which verged on laughter, that reaction did not go unnoticed.

"Scared, James?"

"No." He winced at the weak edge in his voice and cleared his throat. *"No."*

Better.

"I am just amazed at your inaccuracy if that little rhyme was meant for me," he said.

Nathaniel sniggered, an unpleasant sound like mucus gathered in the sinus's, tilting his head in expectation of an explanation.

"My parents are alive and well, I have no sister and I'm Welsh, half Welsh anyway. So you failed on each verse."

He couldn't quite recall Wales. In fact he couldn't recall anything but here.

"Poor me," Nathaniel snorted "or poor you...?"

James ignored him; everything seemed as fine as it could be. He hadn't gnawed his hand off or made any other unpleasant mess.

And supper had passed and the agonies of force feeding had long been accomplished.

Like with Silas he was bemused at how the other knew his name but this time he did not question it, he would get no sensible answer.

"James, James, James…" Nathaniel shook his head, "you see less than I do, my time is running and yours is near through."

Turning abruptly James walked out and slammed the door, leaving the man laughing behind him, the sound turning into a malicious growl the further he went.

• • •

The older attendant looked over expectantly as James re-entered, a small smile appearing as he saw the flushed cheeks and flustered appearance.

"He's alive if that is what you want to hear," James muttered tersely, his uncovered eye sparkling in annoyance, "and thank you kindly for not warning me."

"No, I would have preferred to hear the opposite," the man answered, wrinkling his nose "and I said not to go easy on him. Best thing is to ignore the disgusting thing. He makes guesses and hones in if he feels he's cottoned on to something, that's all."

James scowled and sat back down, ignoring the chuckles that emanated from the others direction.

"He's as brainless as the rest of them idiots."

Feeling his heart tighten in annoyance James gripped the handle of the mug more firmly, so much so that the handle made as if to snap.

The comment had been for him that he was certain, but it wasn't worth the energy of retorting.

Instead he swallowed the now cold tea and pushed away from the table, giving a scathing look to those behind him.

"I'm going to do my checks."

If anyone replied he did not hear it, striding away purposefully and back into the corridors.

Chapter Four

So many tales had passed from the lips of those within, flowing as freely as the tears from eyes that would seldom see the mainland again.

Stories of ghosts and dreadful deeds that would make the strongest stomach turn; from mournful spectres to vengeful spirits whose wrath raged like the storms in the heavens.

James had never seen such a visage but as he wandered in the murk and gloom he could see how they came about, almost believe that there was more than what they saw.

And of course, the way the dead were treated would not help. The unclaimed bodies were not committed to the earth with the proper rites and instead were burnt in the flames of a bonfire beyond the walls.

Their ashes left to be taken by the four winds, far and away.

The very building seeped with malice and suffering and even a disbeliever would feel as if unseen eyes were watching as they walked.

Even James was not immune to that sensation, one he would feel constantly unless he distanced himself and became engrossed in focusing his thoughts of other things.

It was a soft weeping that broke his train of thought, quieter than the mice that tiptoed about the floors. It would have been easy to miss but in the silence it was obvious to a sharp ear.

Frowning, the young attendant looked about him, at a loss as to where the sound was coming from; it seemed to have no obvious direction as if it bounced from wall to wall like the haphazard flight of a moth.

He continued on his round with some apprehension as the crying seemed to follow every step he took.

The sound was suddenly overtaken by the sound of approaching footsteps from behind him, James turned to see the unmistakable figure of Dr Morbridge striding without a care down the corridor, flicking violently through his papers as he drew nearer.

"Good evening, Sir," James greeted as the man started to pass him by without any sign of acknowledgment.

"I don't see what is so good about it," the man ejected viciously, his eyes sharply moving to him. "I've had two wretches die today, even in death they make life miserable to all those around them."

"We cannot avoid the reaper," James said casually, "but I suppose the deaths would explain the weeping I heard."

"Weeping?" Morbridge arched an eyebrow "I heard no sorrow for these. Nor should there be any."

"Oh," the other paused, looking awkward as the heavy gaze impaled him, radiating energy, living heat, "perhaps it was a patient then, or a mere mistake of my ears."

The doctor eyed him fixedly for some time before nodding slowly and deliberately.

"I see. Well, do inform me if such things continue, I am I always fascinated with how the mind works and of course finding new specimens."

"I, Sir, am *not* a specimen," James retorted, bristling at the words, "and although I detest saying it you have plenty of them in here."

Morbridge gave what was reminiscent of a grin or a snarl, his teeth somewhat yellow from age and neglect.

"Those I use for study are in need of medical attention, you, I hope, are in better shape than those *unfortunate* souls who I tend to."

He gave a snort of apparent amusement before continuing on his way, not interested in hearing any response James might have.

Had he waited he would have been disappointed for the other man made no attempt at retorting; his eyes sparkled angrily but his tongue stilled itself.

There was little time to think over the vexation. As the footsteps faded the weeping grew louder once again.

Sighing in frustration James disregarded it as best as he could which was not an easy task since it almost seemed as if it the sound was confined inside his very head.

But it was the only option, ignore and hope it would eventually die down.

Thinking logically, it had to be one of the patients, but the cry sounding feminine which threw that into doubt. There were no females in this section; they were all confined at the opposite end, well away from the males.

He moved down the corridor, attempting to cast the pained sobs back wherever they originated from and hoping the continuation of his job would take nullify them in his mind as least. Some unorthodox part of him almost wanted an unruly patient.

But they all seemed quiet, sitting either motionless or rocking gently, their eyes as empty as they felt their lives were.

His feet paused by the last room, Silas's area, and checked through the hatch, nonplussed to see the man was still lying on the bed, tossing the paper as if he had never ceased.

Instead of walking away James's hand reached for his keys and unlocked the heavy door, pushing it open with a wailing screech.

Silas did not flinch at the sound or the intrusion, continuing the rhythmic motion, throw and catch, throw and catch, over and over.

"Good evening, Mr Grey, always the pleasure."

Catching the paper, he crumpled it further in his slender fingers before flicking it away, uncaring of where it would land, and shifting himself into a sitting position. He tilted his head and looked at the other with expectant, curious eyes.

James did not return the half sarcastic greeting, too preoccupied with his own thoughts for the words to register.

"Do you hear strange sounds in here, Mr Everett?"

Take aback by the abruptness and suddenness of the question Silas said nothing for a moment, blinking in bemusement before giving a complaisant smile.

"One hears all sorts of peculiar sounds in such a place," he answered casually. "In the day, overnight, under night..."

24

"Under night?"

"I have too much time on my hands; I make up my own little words and phrases."

"I see. Well to be more specific have you ever heard sobbing? Sobbing that sounds distinctly like a female?"

Silas looked unperturbed by the oddness of the elaboration and instead he chuckled lowly.

"So many tales drift through these walls they are like a constant mist. Tales of those who remain long after the physical body expired; perhaps the thought of freedom that can never be realised keeps them on."

James looked dubious. When it came to such things he was cynical, unless he experiences or saw something that he was unable to disprove.

"Imagination runs wild under such conditions," he stated flatly as if trying to quell his own nerves "I am fairly certain that was all it was. Stories and speculation just add to anxiety, lead to the instability of a mind."

Silas gave a listless shrug and dropped back onto his bed.

"You asked me, I answered," he said as he gazed back at the crack in the ceiling. "You can believe me or believe me not."

"I wouldn't say you gave an answer, just a ramble," James huffed, leaning against the door. Most would have added that what could one expect from someone incarcerated in a madhouse? But James would not, and if he was about to, Silas spoke before.

"Well, if you want a concise answer, then no. I haven't noticed as such but as I stated one hears so many sounds that they go over your head." Lazy eyes turned slowly. "It isn't uncommon to mistake the call of birds for the weeping of a human. Perhaps they are mimicking the actions we are forbidden."

His idle gaze picked up the downcast expression that appeared briefly on the others face, a matter of seconds, before he assumed his normal stoic one.

"This is a place where the mind can easily have jests played upon it, it isn't to say you're," he paused, giving a sniff of amusement, "losing your sanity."

25

"Something I indeed wish to avoid," he tapped a blunted nail on his thumb, bitten down rather than trimmed judging by the raggedness of the edge.

"Try closing your eyes and counting slowly to ten, I've heard that can work," Silas suggested. "Apparently focussing your mind on such a banal objective takes its focus from what you are concerned about."

"Worth a try, thank you."

He fell into a stagnant silence, feeling the weight of the green eyes on him. For some strange reason this didn't bother him as much as it ought to have done, nor did the fact he was standing in the same room as someone certified as insane.

But Silas...Silas was far more placid and seemed far more stable than the others who he checked on, their souls as empty as their eyes.

Broken dolls that feared their mender.

James looked down at his watch, he'd dallied long enough and if anyone happened by the consequences were not something he'd welcome.

"I had best go but I'm sure I will see you again."

"Of course. Do write before you drop by, after all I'm *dreadfully* busy and have a rather full schedule, darling."

James couldn't hold back the chuckle which resonated around the room; hurriedly he bit his lip. It wouldn't do to run the risk of having someone hear.

He gave a cursory smile and left without another word, the door sounding violently behind him. The papers he held seemed damp, or was it just his palms?

'James..?'

James stiffened, halting his walk down the corridor. He didn't want to turn around, the sound of discernible words more fear inducing than the woeful weeping.

He shifted, prolonging the turn as long as he could; there was no way of continuing without assuring himself it was the result of an overactive imagination.

The woman was on the taller side, her curves perfectly fitting the red dress with wore under the sheer top.

It was short. Cut above the knees, something that was apparently seen in the seedy surroundings of a backstreet brothel. At least if the words of his colleagues could be believed.

Her sandaled feet were reddened from the cold, the rest of her skin pale as though drained of its life's blood.

She looked at him; her limpid eyes were set deep and were pleading as she held out a white hand, urging him to take hold of it.

James backed away.

Although too solid for any spectre it was clear by the aura she exuded that she was not of this world. Or not of his world anyway.

Seeing him start to retreat she lifted her other slender arm, seeming desperate to clutch him to her. And at that James wrenched open the nearest door, not caring where it led, and fled through it.

The woman watched, tears slowly coursing down her cheek as she faded away like the mist on a summer morning.

• • •

James leant against the cold metal of the door, his breath coming in ragged, panicked gasps, his heart pounding wildly in his breast.

He felt light headed and the cold surroundings swayed nauseatingly before his eyes, the vision seeming hazy.

Closing his eyes he slowly counted to ten, taking the advice not long given, feeling relief wash over him as he opened them to sense that all had returned to normal.

'It had to be an inmate, a lock must have broken,' he thought logically to himself 'the face seemed somewhat familiar.'

The doorway he had retreated through had led to long, empty corridor, leading down towards the female quarters.

It was an area that the men rarely set foot in unless the common issue of the monthly curse turned to hysteria that the matron was unable to control.

Ever there but seldom frequented it had taken on a musty, dank stench like an abandoned basement.

With much trepidation James turned back to ease open the door again, the hinges screeching at the slowness and pressure of the movement.

Nothing.

Nothing but the soft whisper of the wind outside and the dismal brightness from the moon that resembled the face of a dying maiden beyond the trees.

Chapter Five

The next few days passed in quiet, monotonous fashion, all merging into one long headache. This was increased when the only sounds the ears heard were constant metallic bangs and piercing screeches of unknown origin.

The evening had hit another lull in activity and having finished the normal checks James lingered to speak with Silas again.

No one was around, the others keeping well away from their charges now they had finished their act of charity by making sure they still lived.

Silas was sat languidly on the chair near his desk, toying with a thread he had pulled from his shirt cuff; the buttons had long been removed in case he attempted suicide by choking on one.

"I am fortunate I was not considered an esteemed individual, had I have been this may have been in the papers and God knows what distasteful things I would have been accused of," he sighed, draping the cotton on the desk. "My good name tarnished by malicious speculation."

James shifted from his position at the door.

"Do you really not know why you are here?"

"My dear fellow I have my doubts that any of us do, you certainly don't."

James's eyes glazed momentarily with irritation, bristling at the remark.

"I work here!" His tone was indignant. "There can be no aspersions cast upon me!"

Silas shook his head, his lips twisting into a smile of both pity and disdain. There was uncertainty in the others words which his sharp ears noted even if the other didn't.

"Mind's eyes, James."

He turned his attention back to the white fibre, apparently done with the subject as his words became lighter.

"You know I used to be an expert this knots and ties," Silas chuckled lowly. "I especially had a flair with corsets, no one was able to get them tighter than I was, although," he studied his nails, "it wreaked havoc on these."

The attendant gave him a withering look while attempting not to chuckle himself. The other frowned, tilting his head incredulously.

"Why is it that I always appear to be a figure of fun?" he said with an air of exasperation. "I'm surprised they don't display us like zoo animals and have people pay to gawk at us."

James cleared his throat and regained himself.

"I have the feeling that that wouldn't be beyond some people's way of thinking but since this location is hardly accessible to the average traveller then it is impossible."

"Then perhaps I should think myself fortunate in other ways also."

Silas idly played with a lock of his long hair, plaiting it dexterously before undoing it in similar fashion.

"Did you find the source of the sounds you heard?" he suddenly asked in blasé tone. "Weeping was it not?"

James felt as though icy tendrils wrapped about his heart at the recollection of that evening, the memory of the form that seemed so real and yet could not have been.

"No," he answered as indifferently as he could "I suspect it was imagination or just a misunderstanding. As you said the sounds of the birds are so seldom heard that it is easy to think of them as something else. I am just glad superstition does not run rife here, otherwise they would see it as a sign of witchery or to do with my eyes."

Silas nodded, making a hum of agreement before silence fell within the room. Well read, he knew the tales of what people called 'ghost eyes'.

"I had best leave, I won't be popular if I'm discovered loitering," James said before giving a slight sniff of amusement. "Less popular I should say."

The emerald eyes shifted from the silver hair and fixed themselves upon the other, a steady gaze that would make most quiver with unease despite the almost kindly glow they cast.

James waited, sensing the man had more to say but instead he gave a lengthy blink before turning his back. Whatever words he had contemplated speaking would remain unsaid and stored in the vast library of thoughts within.

Giving a nod James departed, closing the door as quietly as possible before returning to his own space to try and persuade his fatigued body to unwind.

The world about him seemed to have frozen again, no movement or sound existed in the gloom save for the little that he himself made as he climbed the stairs.

As if the universe had become trapped in time or forgotten that it existed.

He tried not to let this odd stillness disconcert him too much and shut the door to his room firmly, the dust that had settled upon the sparse furniture billowing up in a small cloud. He rolled his eyes, he had put off dusting for some time and apparently he could not get away with it much longer.

Lowering himself onto his bed James felt his muscles protest. After being cramped and stiff from the constant standing and stress they were unwilling to lessen the tautness.

After a few moments and a few curse words he finally managed to settle himself. Turning his head he noticed the letter he had neglected to open for some days, or had it just arrived? He couldn't recall.

Reaching over he took hold of the creased envelope and looked for a postmark to find some indication of where it was from or maybe a name or initials scrawled on the back.

But there was nothing, just his name inscribed on the front and the name of the asylum; it was a wonder it even arrived.

Pushing his finger into the seal James opened it, casting the envelope aside where it fell with a soft rustle.

Unfolding the enclosed paper he blinked in bemusement, staring in both confusion and concern at the contents.

It was a drawing, clearly created by the hand of a child; the lines were shaky as they made a conscious effort to be careful and in turn made their fingers shake all the more.

Four figures adorned the white background, a man and woman with their children. The girl was the perfect image of her mother while the boy resembled the father. Only with mismatched eyes, the only colours in the picture.

As innocuous as the picture seemed it sent chills through him.

'Coincidence,' James thought, swallowing the lump that had formed in his throat, 'or some juvenile prank my colleagues see fit to play. One would think they hadn't anything better to do than irritate me.'

His gaze remained on the image for a while until the growing headache made him look away. Scrunching it up into a ball he tossed it heedlessly into the bin, why torment himself with it?

Sitting up with a sigh he opened the drawer and looked at the blade he kept, it gave a sense of security like one would have with a dog by their side, knowledge that if need be protection was there.

'I could say this is another puzzle,' James thought as he touched the cold handle. 'I cannot remember where I obtained this. Whether it was a gift or something I got myself.'

There was a hint of a memory in his mind, as fleeting as a flake of snow in summer.

He closed the drawer with a sharp snap. There was no point in dredging in the dark to find an answer to an unimportant question. Or chasing an answer that he perhaps did not want to discover.

His eyes drifted back to the crumpled paper which was slowly unfurling in the corner where it lay. A strange feeling washed over him, a feeling of something long sealed away, something that was beginning to escape.

He flopped back against the flat pillow, groaning in unison with the springs, and covered his eyes with his hand.

"God help those who see fit to help others..."

James must have fallen asleep for when he uncovered his eyes and checked his watch over an hour had elapsed even though it felt like seconds.

He blinked, confused as to where he was for a moment until his thoughts had gathered again and the impending checks came to the forefront.

Sitting up slowly he reached for the drawers to steady himself as he got to his feet but his hand touched another surface.

The drawing.

The paper was creased from being opened out and made the smiling faces seem wrinkled and unfriendly, their eyes taunting him.

Something seemed different, the older figures oddly faded as if they were disappearing, their lips appearing slanted as though the smiles were fading to frowns or fear.

James fumed to himself, not only at the fact the image was there but at the sheer audacity that his colleagues had. That was the only thing it could have been, someone sneaking into his room just to fool about.

He was even more annoyed that his own guard had been so lax that he had not heard their footfall on the floorboards.

He dashed the picture to the floor again; he would shred or burn the blasted thing later when his shift was finished.

Muttering nonsensically to himself, nonsense that even he couldn't comprehend, he pulled himself to his feet and stalked from the room purposefully.

• • •

James barely noticed where he was walking, his annoyance too great to take anything more in than that which was directly in front of him. Had it not been for the knowledge that he would most likely break his neck on the stairs he probably would have not registered that either.

The scent of damp, and muted sounds from behind the stone walls, brought him back to reality along with the normal leaden feeling in his stomach, the suffering and burden of others brought him down as well.

The handle to the main corridor was cold, as if a tormented soul had frozen it with its touch. He shivered as he pushed it open.

Upon doing so his eyes caught sight of one of his colleagues heading towards the staff areas, purposefully ignoring any who tried to catch his attention.

"If you see your *friends*," James said clearly as he proceeded down the corridor "tell them I'm not amused."

The man blinked before looking scornful as he continued.

"The locks on the door may have long been removed but I don't appreciate uninvited guests playing ridiculous japes."

"No one's been near your room, Grey," the other stated coldly as he turned to continue on his way. "We're indentured servants and have better things to do than toy with you."

"Well clearly someone has! And it has certainly never stopped you in the past." James leant beside the door, his visible eye sparkling with irritation. "Perhaps if you bloody idiots actually *did* your job you'd not have the time!"

The man's face went a dark crimson, furious at the slur. No words were issued as he flounced through the door, swinging it shut behind him and trapping James's fingers in the process with a dull thud.

James swore and yanked his hand back, biting his lip, the knuckles already beginning to bruise, turning a subtle purple that would darken to indigo later.

"Git..."

The word went unheard but provided a release of tension at the very least as he opened the door with his other hand and headed into the all-consuming shadows once again.

Chapter Six

No trouble tainted the rest of the evening, each minute passing slowly and painfully until the day finally broke.

Silence would be his master for some time.

James found he couldn't really remember however many days elapsed so he thought it correct to assume they had been fine even with the dull ache that had throbbed in his fingers which had slowly faded along with the bruising.

But whilst pain and memory faded, the feeling of tension and unease increased; he felt eyes everywhere both from the others and from where no eyes should be.

From the twisted boughs beyond the iron bars, from the dank depths of the courtyard well, but it was foolish to think it.

The idiotic pranks had frayed his already taut nerves and James vowed they would not snap he could not afford to allow them to.

Unable to sleep that morning he had wandered down to the dining area thinking that at least the dull hum of the conversation would alleviate the stresses he felt throbbing in his temples.

He had barely reached the dark double doors before he felt a hand clamp down on his shoulder blade.

Looking round he saw the face of the man who had crushed his fingers, at least he thought it was. The faces all seemed the same and as time went on it became harder to tell who was who.

"You may want to find a better way of getting my attention," James said coldly, his exposed eye glittered like a snowflake in the sunlight. "I could have hit you."

The man smirked, clearly unbothered by the idle threat.

James continued, "And if you want me to do anything then let me firmly state I'm off duty, I'm not running errands to check on patients for you, especially certain ones."

"If you mean old Atrocity, he's fine, unfortunately, sat rambling to himself as usual," the other answered in cruel amusement. "So unless you want to go down there's no obligation."

"I'd rather not, thank you."

"Can't ignore that forever, he's on your list later," the man snorted, "but since you're awake you can take a folder down to the matron in the female quarters, somehow got mixed up with our lot."

Although not forbidden, a man going to the female area felt unseemly and James hesitated, it was not just due to inappropriateness either.

The matron was a ferocious, thin woman with a sharp tongue to match her eyes which were blue and piercing, placed deep into a face lined before its time.

But she was just a woman, even if she sent the stomach roiling, and all he would need to do was to hand over the papers with few words, besides the normal pleasantries, spoken.

"Very well, but next time I need some help I expect the same consideration."

"We'll see. Depends what you want."

He turned and had vanished through the door before James could retort, the first thing springing to mind was not practically breaking his fingers.

Giving a groan of annoyance he made his way back the direction he had come to follow the winding way into the female's area, bypassing the kitchen and seldom used main hall, it's recreational purpose long forgotten.

Other than the rooms being occupied by the female sex there was no marked difference in the layout and the surroundings were just as grey and drab.

A strong ammoniacal odour came wafting forward from some of the unfortunates, their bodies no longer able to perform even the basic functions and they were left to sit in their own waste. The closets used for relieving oneself were in better order.

James kept his eyes forward like a disinterested soldier, viewing the women in this state made him feel as if he was an unintentional voyeur to their misery and there was naught they could do to conceal themselves.

The clothing they were given was modest but became frayed and thin over time which often left little to the imagination.

It was the sound of scuffling that caught his attention.

Loud in the deathly silence it reminded him of when he had heard a rat nesting in the walls above his bed.

In the still of the night it had been louder than thunder.

James continued towards the sound, his mingled concern and curiosity spurring him forward.

• • •

Marianne was mute.

Her lips would move but no protest passed them but her eyes spoke well enough to betray her agonies and fear of the male who stood over her like an ogre.

She had been discovered in the basement of her home, cowering in the corner rocking herself, her arms wrapped about her shivering body.

A wire lay nearby and a few feet away were the remains of what had once been a developing child, now a gory mess on the stone.

The woman's own wrists dripped a steady flow of crimson where she had attempted to dig deep enough with the blunted point. She bore the scars of many other injuries inflicted upon herself, whether of her own making or another's remained unknown.

She shook her head wildly when accused of aborting the babe, her hands gesticulating in attempts to communicate.

But without words she had no alibi, no reason and the evidence was weighty.

No protest was made from her widowed father when she was hauled away, stating only she had acted in a whorish fashion since puberty and this came as little surprise.

The orderly looked around as James appeared in the half open doorway, releasing the auburn locks he had wrenched up, hurling her back into the wall.

"What the devil are you doing here, Grey?"

"I needed to give the matron some papers; I suspect *your* reasons are less innocent. I suggest you leave the poor woman alone or I will be forced to report your conduct."

"Thank the Gods you are no judge," the other hissed as he stepped away from the prone figure, "crime would thrive, you are as much as a lunatic as these confined with the way you sympathise with them."

"I am most certainly not," James answered staunchly, meeting the sullen eyes. "I simply feel there are other ways to treat people, especially a female who cannot offer defence."

"Then the stupid creature should have learnt to write."

The man shoved him aside forcefully, striding away audibly.

Rubbing his arm James waited until the footsteps had been consumed by the darkness before moving to help Marianne to her feet, her step ungainly from the wasted muscle of her once shapely legs.

It was obvious that she had been a beauty in her days of freedom but strain and fear had sunken and paled her once vibrant features, her skin now painted with bruises and her blonde hair brassy. The dimples that had been so charming in healthier times were now pin pricks on a thinner and tired face.

His heart ached for her; he couldn't imagine this woman had callously slaughtered an innocent in cold blood but he knew all too well that appearances could be deceptive.

Leading her to the bed he sat her on the thin mattress, it provided no comfort but it was better than the floor.

With a small smile he turned to leave, as he did so he felt Marianne studying him intently. It was an off-putting feeling.

"Just because I have no voice does not mean I cannot speak."

James froze as he reached for the door as the feminine voice filled his head but did not register in his ears as sound should.

Swallowing the fear stinging every nerve he turned back around.

Marianne was smiling. Her eyes bright and alive.

She indicated to her forehead with a slender hand and once again a voice filled the man's mind.

"There are ways beyond words."

Giving a slow bow of her head she pulled her thin legs up to her chest and shifted to face the wall, gazing at it as if the blank stone was covered in the most glorious imagery.

James remained rooted to the spot, powerless to command his legs to move. Marianne looked over her shoulder and placed a finger to her lips.

Fumbling wildly for his keys he slammed them into the lock and hastily retreated, briefly, as the door swung shut, her voice returned.

'I was innocence corrupted...'

Clutching the folder to his chest James walked away as swiftly as he dared to locate the matron and get away from the area.

Surely her voice would not carry beyond the walls of her room?

Had it been his shift he would have made his way to speak with Silas again, finding the strange man oddly comforting but it wasn't worth the risk.

People had enough against him without the rumour of fraternising with the insane added to it.

• • •

"Have you heard of Marianne?" James asked Silas later once his checks were done. He wasn't expecting much of an answer considering the segregation rules but word had its way of being passed around.

Hearsay or not any information was useful.

The man looked up from his desk.

"The mute woman? Indeed." He brushed back a lock of his lengthy silver hair. "Why do you ask?"

"No particular reason, I met her today when I had to venture to the females' ward, that's all."

He moved to perch himself on the bed, it was easier than standing around and far less conspicuous if someone happened to recheck.

"You lie, my friend, had there been no reason you would not have inquired."

James gave a small chuckle.

"I don't think I would ever be able to get anything past you. Well, do you find anything *unusual* about her?"

Silas lost his bored expression and smiled with amusement.

"I take it you're referring to her manner of conversing with people; it is rather astounding, though I do feel for the poor girl."

"What do you know of her?" James persisted, curious to know more about the odd female.

"About as much as you probably do, I have had scarcely no interaction with her," Silas sat back, pressing his fingers together to feel the nails dig into the tips "I suggest if you are interested then address her; she need not be in the same room talk. I'm not certain how far she can project her voice but we chinwag every now and then."

"I thought you said you knew as much as I did?" James frowned.

"I do, if you have heard what is passed around, we 'talk' if you like but she never divulges much."

"I see, well since I may not be in that area again for some time perhaps you suggest it to her?"

Silas nodded agreeably, watching as James got to his feet, uncomfortable even on the softer mattress.

"What exactly *do* you discuss if you don't mind my asking?"

"She doesn't say much," Silas paused, a small frown creasing his brow as he bit back the incorrect laughter, "apologies, tactless of me. Anyway, usual trivial chitchat. Futility of existence, boredom, issues with those housed opposite, hardly Plato."

"Not the weather?" James grinned, gestured to the barred windows which the sun rarely squeezed through. "You surprise me, Mr Everett, not asking a lady about how she finds such glorious sunshine."

A rumbling chuckle echoed from the others throat and he clapped a hand to his forehead.

"How *dreadfully* impertinent of me! Perhaps I should invite the dear lady for a stroll along the promenade also."

James laughed, loudly coughing to disguise the sound as it reverberated out of the room.

"Well if you do then remember to tie your hair back," he said after he had regained his breath, "you could throttle someone with it."

"Yes, they wanted to cut it, the attendant nearly lost his eyes," Silas eyed his lengthy nails "these come in useful. But now they only serve to braid my hair, one of the only distractions one has here."

The action had not gone down well, the damage was not exactly minor but the man had money and that held high value.

Solitary confinement was all that was dealt out.

James moved to the door, time didn't stand still no matter how much it seemed to lag and he had dallied enough.

"I have to go, is there anything you need?"

"Apart from the obvious?" The reply was terse. "Freedom? Company? Choices of my own? No."

It had been a foolish question, one that had served only to irritate for what could he really do for him that held any worth?

Chapter Seven

I once walked where the wild roses grew,
Over grasses covered with mist and dew.
But now my dreams are nought but pain
And how I long to wake again.

Strange lights flickered, emitting an odd humming sound as if a swarm of insects danced within them.

There was so much white.

White walls, white bedding, it was almost blinding.

The floor however was a sickly green, made worse from the glow above, elongated shadows stretched from under the bed like the monsters feared in childhood.

James sat up.

Automatically his arms embraced his body, it was cold. The thin nightshirt he was wearing gave no true warmth.

In the silence his heart sounded like voodoo drum.

'This cannot be real. A lucid dream...'

Slowly he fingered the clothing, moving to touch the coarse blanket. It felt real. Even the most vivid of dreamlands could not replicate everything in the physical world.

Swallowing his fear he turned, drawn by the subtle shimmer of a photo frame standing idly on the bedside cabinet.

Smiling faces of a couple and two children greeted his gaze.

The image was in colour, something he had never seen before, as if they had been cut from real life and confined into a small portrait prison.

Falling back onto the bed James closed his eyes, so tightly it felt as though the lids themselves would tear, and counted out loud.

"One...two...three..."

All the way up to ten.

With sickness rising threateningly in his throat James slowly reopened his eyes, the feeling receding, washed away with relief as he was met with the view of the shoddy, bleak surroundings.

Which now looked like Eden on earth.

Looking out of the small barred window he saw a sliver of red seep through the dense boughs to herald the dusk.

The birdsong, such as it was, was dying and becoming even more muted by the thick foliage.

'I cannot risk trying to sleep any longer,' James thought as he returned to the welcome warmth of the blanket, pulling it over his legs as he leant against the wall, 'but after that I fear sleep will be hard to succumb to anyway.'

But the toll of work had caught up and he could not fight the drowsiness, his body feeling as if it was made of lead and soon he slipped into an uneasy slumber.

Chapter Eight

Letters from the outside world arrived very seldom.

When they did arrive, it was just as rare that they found their way to the person to whom they were addressed.

Under Morbridge's orders each was scrutinised for unsuitable content, any items sent were confiscated, stolen or hidden away where they became fodder for the rats.

Most patients became too far gone to care about word from outside. Bitterness was strong and was directed at their families for abandoning them there to begin with.

If they had been forgotten it came as no surprise.

And what better way to keep the belief that they were worth nothing?

Keep the control over their lives since they had no one else and nowhere else but the cold walls that surrounded them.

The letters that did eventually get past the keen eye of the doctor and staff were left to a ragged hessian sack until, and if, the warders decided to distribute them.

Mostly due to the money paid to the asylum Silas was often the only one privileged enough to receive the letters which were few and far between.

Once they had been almost weekly but they now dwindled.

"Who are these from, if you don't mind me asking?" James said as he handed a rather dog-eared envelope to the long nailed male on his next round.

"Partner," Silas looked lazily at the handwriting, setting it aside on the desk for later, adding with a low chuckle, "I live in sin if you listen to the bigoted blather of the holy. But if you consider my life in general I have been damned since my birth."

James smiled tightly, his breath hitching in his throat, uncertain on what, if any, response he could give.

Silas seemed not to notice, dropping into his seat and leaning back with a thoughtful expression.

"However it is as I have always said, no one is truly sane, not even God. For if He was then why would He have created mankind? And in his image no less?"

"You would probably have been hung for saying that years ago, even today you would cause uproar."

"Why do you think the chaplain never comes anymore?" Silas cocked his head, smirking. "Could not cope with our dreadfully sacrilegious views. Honestly, the man would not be satisfied if we were all identical copies of Jesus Christ himself."

"Yes," James said noncommittally, scratching the back of his neck. He shifted his attention to his list, the papers filling the awkward silence with a soft rustle like the leaves in autumn.

Upon seeing Nathaniel written crudely below Silas, obviously the normal staff member was ill or merely wanted to avoid that particular patient.

"I must take my leave, I hope your letter brings you good news or at least some comfort that you have one who thinks fondly of you."

Silas nodded casually, making no move to take up the envelope, at least not whilst James was present.

Even as the attendant left only his eyes moved to towards it. The last letter had been short with banal and repetitive content.

He couldn't help but feel dread that it would be the case again and fear that it would be the bearer of more unpleasant news.

Waiting would not alter the contents and the procrastination would only increase anxiety but he could not bring himself to touch it.

He turned away, letting it lie.

• • •

Nathaniel was eerily quiet as James entered, the only sound his calm breathing along with the others footfall.

James could tell he was not sleeping though, he felt the heavy gaze in his direction even through the blindfold the man wore.

And his index finger tapped idly on his black clad thigh.

As oppressive as the silence was, he continued the checks, there were not many in the lower rooms since the few patients that were there were often force fed and the water was not left.

Their surroundings greying and empty.

Turning to leave James froze mid-step, his heart palpitating as he heard the chains that bound the man rattle ominously.

He found himself unable to move and could only pray that the next sound would not be that of the iron falling to signify they had failed in their duty.

Instead he heard the deep growling voice, the one that had been the last sound in so many ears, utter only four words.

"Behold the Titanium Ghost…"

James shifted around, his movement as graceless as a figure on a dying musical box and stared at the man in confusion. The words made no sense yet still they dripped with malice.

Much like their first conversation.

This time he didn't rise to it.

Slowly he took a step back, his focus remaining on the other, feeling their eyes meet as he gripped the door.

Nathaniel smiled a cruel smirk that would have matched his expression had it been viewable. Even bound and blind he held his power.

Time seemed to stand still for a moment as the two regarded each other, deathly silence fell and not even the twitch of the keys broke it.

Nathaniel suddenly yanked his arm down, the crash of chains shattering the atmosphere like a breaking mirror.

He laughed maliciously as he heard the other jolt and flee the room, his hastened footsteps fading at he mounted the stairs.

• • •

'Behold the Titanium Ghost.'

What on earth had that meant?

James hadn't a clue and the words dwelled in his mind as he slowly returned to his quarters, heart gradually calming from the frantic beat.

But, when he considering the way Nathaniel was, had they meant anything except to the man himself?

That was what the others would say; brush it off like dust on their clothing. But James wasn't sure; something deep within him sensed that it mattered.

He felt cold, colder than normal, and shuddered.

• • •

Marianne sat still on her bed, her posture stiff as if she were a porcelain doll awaiting the return of its owner, her blue eyes just as glassy.

It was the position she took when lost in conversation with another.

Her lips twitched in a small smile as she heard the request from Silas, she had hoped James would be curious enough about her skills to ask her to 'speak' more.

She hadn't been permitted to be sociable in the outside world, her muteness an embarrassment. What man would even look at a woman who had no voice, no talent? Her parents described her as 'just a trinket to hang upon one's arm'.

Then the baby. That had been the coup de grace which had sealed her fate and confined her to this cell.

The scenery changed but people didn't. They were cruel, disinterested and saw her as a burden and little more.

They had told her she was there as charity instead of being cast onto the streets likes an unwanted canine; she would accept what was done for her and be grateful.

But it was hard to accept when one was given next to nothing.

Returning to the conscious world, Marianne dropped back onto the mattress, breathing in its musty, damp scent. A smell that

47

should have turned the stomach but had become one of security for most of the patients.

A tear welled up in her eye, finally escaping and leaving a silver trail on her cheek.

• • •

James was lying on his own bed, feeling the lumps in the mattress dig into his back and watching a cobweb drift idly to and fro in the corner of the ceiling.

Occasionally his eyes drifted down to the floor to where the drawing lay. He had once again crumpled it and tossed it aside but felt the strange urge to check and make sure it was still in that state.

'It was a foolish joke,' he chided himself as he tore his gaze away, 'it is not worth fraying my nerves over.'

Even so he inched himself over to reach into his drawer to touch the cool metal of the knife that lay within.

The feel of it sent a small sense of security through him. He allowed his fingers to linger a while before pulling back.

'Think of me and I shall hear.'

James frowned as the words echoed in his skull, making his temples ache. How odd that a soft feminine voice could cause such pains.

It felt as bad as the migraines he was prone to getting, albeit shorter.

He tried to picture the wan-looking woman, the once handsome features but as he did so he happened to look to the corner.

The picture was unravelled and looking back were the four crudely drawn figures. His mind immediately lost the image of Marianne and instead recalled the strange woman in the corridor.

The cartoonish eyes seemed to stare at him, seemed to see him, *through* him.

James debated whether to get up and tear the damned picture into pieces but something held him back, the inanimate gaze making him apprehensive about picking it up yet alone shredding it.

'If I leave it I'll not sleep, I have to move it,' he thought resolutely as he eased himself up. 'It isn't as if it is a living, breathing object.'

Taking a deep breath and ignoring the heavy feeling in his stomach James got to his feet, keeping 'eye contact' with the girl in the picture as he approached. His hands shook as he reached down to pluck the paper from the floor.

Time was forgotten as he stared as if hypnotised at the figures, from the smiling parents to the children, his focus lingering on the boy with the mismatched eyes.

He folded it up with a shudder.

Hopefully shutting it away in his drawer would work better than casting it aside.

Chapter Nine

Much to his disappointment James did not hear Marianne's voice again that evening. It was perhaps not surprising, fear and anxiety had rendered him incapable of focusing enough to channel to her.

He was mulling over ways to clear his head the next day over what was said to be tea but quite frankly tasted more like stale dishwater.

"Where did you put that paper I gave you yesterday, Grey?"

James looked up to meet the eyes of the attendant who had slammed the door on his fingers. He shook his head, looking puzzled.

"What are you talking about? I haven't seen you since you nearly broke my hand."

The man frowned, exasperation evident in his expression.

"That was over a week ago, Grey! You don't even have the bruises to show for it now!" He seized James's hand and pulled it up to show his fingers were healed, only a very faint hint of purple coloured the knuckles.

James jerked his hand back, annoyed by the others audacity but more so by his own memory. He flexed the digits, searching for any residual pain that would prove to him that time had not passed in the way it appeared to have done.

"I suppose I lost track of time," he said quietly, masking his unease, "easy done around here."

"Or you're losing your mind like the rest of them," the man muttered irritably, "and since you appear to have lost your damned memory I assume you can't remember where you put that paper?"

"No. But tell me what it was and I can probably give you an idea about where it might be."

"It was a paper concerning the changes in treatment for some of these idiots. I gave it to since I had to restrain Johnson again."

James could not recall a patient names Johnson let alone where the paper was regarding him. It was as if a thick fog had fallen in his mind and cloaked all memories from the days prior.

"Don't bother." The man held up a rough hand. "I get the feeling that even if you did, you'd conveniently forget."

Before James could offer any retort, the other had gone, striding purposefully and clearly unwilling to stop and converse further.

James remained where he was, the tea rapidly cooling in the chipped mug, it puzzled him. Even people's names seemed lost, perhaps they never told him but somehow he doubted that. Would not everyone tell you their names when you worked with them?

The air about him suddenly felt colder than normal. Noises of humming, faint voice talking in chorus filled his ears.

With sickness once again rising in his stomach he got up to feet, leaving the mug where it was, and hastened from the room, trying to leave the disquiet behind him.

The lower areas held many secrets besides the patients deemed untreatable, too vicious for anything but incarcerating and erasing from memory.

Beyond the dust and gloom of the seldom swept corridors, through the doors whose hinges seemed to scream in agony as they resisted opening was an empty area with a locked entrance to another.

When not in his office or eyeing the patients Morbridge spent much of his time down there. He was far more comfortable in the gloom surrounded in the clinical surroundings.

The room was a normal doctor's nightmare. The filing cabinets disorganised and dusty, the table still stained with the blood of the last luckless occupant. Only the surgical tools were shimmering softly in the scant light.

Morbridge never allowed anyone to clean down there except

himself. The order of information and items was one only he knew and that was how it was to be left.

It was unclear if even the other staff knew of the area's existence.

Dark eyes studied the barely decipherable papers as the doctors' hands carefully polished the blade of the scalpel. He paused, examining the lethal point that had sliced the skin of so many.

Wilson, Elias. Male, white.
Found wandering side streets. No family known.
Mentally defective, claims to hear voices.

To Morbridge such a patient was ideal. With no family ties it was far less troublesome when the patient passed. Although he had found that few relatives would step forward even when they were known to exist, no one wanted madness in the family to taint the bloodline. It was a charitable offer if any did fund the interment of the mortal remains.

He smiled coldly, setting the sparkling instrument aside and gathering the papers, making a mental note of the area number and room. Voices were an issue he came across too often in this field and so far no one had found an appropriate or lasting solution. Morbridge had a few things in mind, if it didn't work it would be no loss and if it did...it would be a highlight on his career.

Extinguishing the lamp with a hiss he left the room, locking the door behind him with the rusted key that screeched in the hole.

His footsteps were almost silent as he made his way towards the staircase but still a sharp ear heard, and a soft but audible chuckle sounded from behind a cell door.

The doctor paused and cast a stony glare that would not be seen by the occupant even had he not been blindfolded.

His keys jangled as he sorted the correct one and flung the door open, filling the air with the cold chill from the corridor.

Nathaniel turned in his direction, a smirk twisting his lips as he recognised the surgical scent that Morbridge would emit intermingled with a musky smell of age.

"Something amuse you, Nathaniel?" Morbridge asked indifferently.

"I would find it astounding anything would unless you're thinking of the wonderfully grotesque mess you made of your acquaintances."

"The skin is so plain, so dull; I created art, not mess."

"I think their family may beg to differ. Especially since a handful were violated," he looked at the other in disgust.

Nathaniel's head rose abruptly, his chains rattling as he pitched himself angrily forward. His muscles tensed under the thin fabric of the clothing as he pulled his restraints.

"I never touched them! I have limits and I shall never cross them!" he ejected furiously, his eyes blazing beneath the blindfold so brightly they could have burnt through. "I despise those who touch and take without consent! And those who butcher children, the innocent babes will not suffer at my hand!"

Morbridge sneered but took an automatic step backwards, a fact that apparently didn't go unnoticed by the other.

"So even a cold heart senses danger. You flaunt yourself as fearless, but are you truly fearless or just foolhardy?

"If I were an idiot I would leave you unrestrained, worthless cur!" Morbridge hissed. "I don't fear you, I only fear being in the presence of a diseased mind that would threaten the cleanliness of my own."

Nathaniel looked away, his silence being more of an insult than words could ever be. Silence fell heavy until the doctor exhaled strongly, leaving the other to his bleak bliss. He had more important issues to attend to and the confrontation had served only to ignite the urgency.

Or at the very least exacerbate his anger towards those in his care.

The door closed with a ferocity that made the walls shake and the sound of the footsteps storming away was joined by the cackle of laugher.

• • •

After some searching in random drawers James had discovered a handful of papers that noted recent changes in treatment in various patients.

He handed them silently to his colleague who thumbed through them carelessly smudging the ink and plucking a sheet out.

"Put them where you can remember," he said as he thrust the others back into James's hands. "The doctor is bad enough but he's allowed to be."

"Double standards. He has less excuse than we have," James mumbled to himself.

"Not our business to question," the other retorted as he turned to leave. "Keep your mind on your job and that alone."

James made no response, pushing the papers back in the drawer; ignoring the look of displeasure he was cast. He had found the papers in there and he would remember they were in the future.

"Now if you'll excuse me my shift isn't until this evening and I don't get paid extra for running errands on my own time."

He slipped deftly past the larger man to fade into the shadows of the passages. Sometimes he wished he could really do that, become one with the nothingness that had been there before nothingness had existed.

• • •

The courtyard was silent.

Beyond the walls and past the trees the ocean was grey and placid, barely a ripple troubling its surface.

Even the breeze seemed non-existent.

James walked carefully over the cobbles, needing whatever air was present. The area often felt warmer than his room as well, sheltered by the towering stone structure.

His destination was the well, to sit on the damp rim and try and empty his mind, throwing his doubts and concerns down to the abyss below to drown in the waters.

As he made drew closer an eerie sound filled his ears. An echoic sobbing which seemed to emanate from the well itself which caused him to falter, his feet seeming to gain lead weights, his steps becoming slow and dragging.

Even so he forged forth, both fearful and fascinated by the cries the well was giving.

His fingers clutched the clammy stone of the lip and slowly he peered over into the dark maws which seemed to gape like a hungry beast.

There was nothing. Just the inky water waving back.

Feeling rather pathetic for letting his imagination get the better of him James sat uncomfortably with a heavy sigh that seemed to echo in the empty space.

'James...'

He stiffened as his ears picked up the faint voice as if the icy breeze had frozen his limbs. He breathed out slowly. He hadn't heard that. It was a foolish fancy. The tales that were often told had clearly had more impact than he had thought.

For a brief moment he recalled Marianne but the voice did not resemble hers.

He turned around stoically and again looked down to be met with the same sight except with a few ripples as droplets of rain began to fall from the corpulent clouds above.

'God damn it,' he cursed inwardly, running his fingers through his hair and casting the clinging drops to join the others.

He could stay there no longer. His need for sanity outweighing his need for the fresh air.

Chapter Ten

Sitting on the stained sheets Marianne rocked herself, a fluid, gentle movement as if rocking a baby into slumber.

Of course she would never compare it to that, not when her mind recalled the bloody creature that had been torn from within her.

A thin blanket covered her shoulders and gave a modicum more dignity and warmth that had been stripped so long ago.

But she knew it could well have been worse. She at least had clothing, albeit skimpy and tattered, some others were not so fortunate.

It should have been provided. A right and not a privilege but still it could be taken and sold since those who it belonged to no longer seemed to care their flesh was bared to the elements. No longer aware of the straw that scratched their blistered skin or the cold of the chains that often bound them.

The cold could be unbearable but one never complained for fear of the beatings they incurred. It was simpler to lose pride instead.

Her thoughts drifted the James. The blond intrigued her and not just because of the strangeness of his fringe that hid his one eye. He had a kind aura. A heart which the others lacked as if they were blind and deaf to suffering.

Maybe they were. Victims of circumstance like the other asylum dwellers, only they had hardened their souls to relieve any guilt that tried to penetrate.

She hummed in her head. A mindless little ditty that gathered her concentration and the energy it took to send her 'voice'.

When in close quarters it was simpler. Attuning her mind to

theirs took little effort if she felt a connection but at a distance it could be taxing until their link was established properly. Silas was so far the only one who she had achieved this with.

And until now the only one she had wanted to.

'Speak to me and I shall hear.'

She cast out the same words as before, her calling card if you will. She hoped James would not dismiss the echo as a dream or his own mind failing him.

• • •

James was tidying what little he had in his room. It had become an almost obsessive habit, one he leant on when his sleep was disturbed.

If there was no dust he would simply shift things about, organising and reorganising. It made a change from pacing or lying studying the ceiling.

It was rare there was no dust though; in fact it often seemed as if the room was a flourishing garden for it.

'Speak to me and I shall hear.'

He paused as the words flowed into his mind, looking around him as if he expected to see her form beside him.

"Marianne?" His voice was soft and tentative.

'Use your mind. Focus on me, my face and voice. I shall hear then.'

James nodded even though she could not see his acknowledgement. Whilst her advice seemed simple it was far more complex than he thought, his mind drifting away from her face to other things that lingered in the background.

Marianne was patient. It was a skill that was difficult for one whose concentration was fraught to master. It was why Silas found it easy; he had nothing more as such to occupy himself with. Perhaps the other inmates would be the same?

She didn't know since she hadn't tried as they were lost to her in their own realities.

She listened carefully, picking up fragments of James's attempts. She appreciated the effort; even incoherent rambling of a fellow patient was a break from the heavy silences.

'It will come. Rest your mind for now and I shall send word to you on the morrow.'

James sighed in annoyance at his inability to focus. He knew it was not entirely his fault but he was a man, he should be able to do what he set his mind upon the first time.

"I shall try to see you again," he muttered, hoping his words made it to her. "I will find reason."

James's voice was faint in her mind, almost covered by the sound of her breathing echoing in the room, but she heard. A smile graced her lips for a tiny moment.

She would indeed look forward to it, another break to her monotonous existence. She sent no word back, doubting that in his obvious tired state he would hear.

Chapter Eleven

The corridor echoed as Morbridge's heavy feet paced the stone. The few attendants he encountered stepped swiftly aside; the man's sharp eyes were not seeing the surroundings and focussed instead on his ideas.

His destination was the main hall. The large empty room used to reward those who had some sense left and were seen to have no risk attached to them.

Those with families and those with money would also benefit.

• • •

The recreation hall was large and open. If fully lit it could almost be described as pleasant. The wooden floor sparkled in the soft lustre of the lights, almost as brightly as the real sun in the outside world. But the sense of freedom outweighed all else. Even the bars on the windows could not take that away completely.

In the corner of the otherwise empty room was a seldom used piano, the keys dusty and the chords tuneless when played. It never seemed to bother those who now and again prodded ebony or ivory. It was a sound that brought images of joy and normality, all the things they lacked.

Few were present.

There were not many deemed trustworthy enough to be allowed to enjoy the facilities or many who the warders decreed as none problematic. They didn't need to be bothered by the issues that haunted and affected even the upper class patients.

Morbridge eyes the scattered individuals. At his right two men fought robotically, their faces surly but their eyes empty. The blows were superficial and inflicted the damage that a feather would to an egg.

He ignored them, as did the attendants; such imbeciles were of little interest and not worth bothering with.

To the doctor the more coherent held more appeal, not those whose minds had departed and whose bodies continued. He could clearly see the changes his treatments brought about, both great and small.

His eyes drifted to a woman sat near the piano. Her frail frame wrapped in a tattered dress and mouldering shawl. Judging by the careful crocheting of the garment she had been talented. His gaze lingered, studying her poise and mannerisms. The hazel orbs were clearly reading the scraps of music, humming the melody that was written.

After a moment he strode over, stopping at what would be considered a polite distance and nodded to her genially as she looked up.

"I don't believe we have met, Madam," he said smoothly, the kind tone blighted by the shark like smile, "but I feel I know you well enough from your notes and your plight touches me. These walls were not meant to contain those such as yourself and I would be delighted if you would allow me to aid you further."

His knowledge of her was brief; left by her husband due to feminine issues. What they were he didn't know or care, hysteria most likely. That was the main reason for the women who were here. But she had been a 'lady' and apparently still saw herself as one despite the conditions she now kept.

"You could get me home?" The female's eyes filled with hope, bright and childlike. "Back to where I should be?"

"Perhaps," Morbridge gave a crooked smirk. "Depends if you are willing to work to better yourself, to take the offer of help. Whatever it may be."

The coldness of the latter words seemed to go unnoticed. The female was desperate to depart from such vile surroundings where the clean and filthy were kept together, the calm and the violent.

It worsened her symptoms, deteriorated her shattered nerves even more.

Offered that shred of hope, the woman could ignore the chill in his words, there was finally a small hint of sunlight in the darkness and whatever treatment she must bear she vowed she could. It meant returning to the arms of her loved ones, removing the disgrace that her incarnation must have caused them.

She accepted the hand that was offered to help her to her feet, following like an obedient puppy, hopeful and wide eyed.

"What is your name, my dear?" Morbridge asked as amiably as he could as led the woman out and down the winding corridor. There was a biting chill in the air which even he could feel and in the thin almost translucent gown she would surely feel it tenfold. "I care for so many unfortunate souls that their names sometimes escape me."

The woman's step was slow and stiff due to the lack of movement and it irked the doctor to slow his own to allow her to keep pace but the benefits outweighed the slight hindrance.

"My name is Abigail…"

"Abigail," Morbridge repeated with a nod as if committing it to memory. "How charming, I always like names that began with A."

She smiled rather shyly in response, unused to compliments or that which resembled them.

"Down here." Morbridge held open the heavy door leading down an iron stairway to the basement rooms below, adding as he moved forward. "Mind your step. There is little light and the steps have no guards."

Abigail nodded as she gripped the railing carefully, the metal cold and clammy beneath her fingers. The passage became darker the further she went and it was only the soft hue of the doctor's white coat that guided her.

Her step began to falter.

"Not far," Morbridge paused to wait impatiently a few paces ahead, "first on the right when you reach the bottom."

He received a hum of acknowledgement. A heavy feeling of trepidation was beginning to weigh the woman down. Every scrap of logic, every fibre of her being was screaming for her to retreat.

As she began to mull over the possibility of turning a strong hand clamped down on her wrist, blunt nails digging into fragile skin.

"Afraid of the dark, girl?" Morbridge smirked. "You know the only monsters are those in your mind."

"I..."

"Hush. Do not fear," he cooed sardonically, silencing whatever words that were about to emerge. "Poor dear, you've been locked in your own little world so long you can't discern help from hindrance."

Abigail stiffened and gave a nervous tug to attempt to free her wrist but the grip remained firm.

The action only seemed to amuse the doctor, bolstering his already inflated ego.

"No, no," he hissed maliciously, pushing open the nearest door, "acceptance is an agreement and an agreement is not to be broken."

The room within was pitch. The centre table lit by a single gaslight hung from a slender chain. It seemed clean with a scent of iodine covering the smell of the coppery blood from a pile of stained sheets concealed in the shadows.

A wire cage sat opposite a disorganised cabinet, large enough to contain a moderately sized dog.

Pushing Abigail forward Morbridge closed the door behind them, the clang sounding to her like the death tolls sounded to the condemned.

"Sit," he said in monosyllabic tone and gestured to a stool near the metal table. "I shall be with you in a moment."

"I'm not sure..."

"Take a seat."

The order was not negotiable.

Abigail swallowed hard; a painful lump had formed in her throat and was choking any words she wanted to voice, coupled with an agonising nausea.

She backed away and sat stiffly, the hard seat pressed painfully into the bones of her backside, the fat long since wasted away.

Morbridge waited until she was seated before moving over, circling like a predator watching its new prey.

He said nothing as he turned away and moved to the cabinet, pulling the drawer open with a loud bang.

"Now. The question is if you are going to cease your mundane chatter and complaints and let me work?" He reached into the dark confines and pulled out a metal object. It resembled a fork, bent in the middle as if melted by an intense heat or worked upon by some sideshow charlatan. Two thin wires were threaded through tiny holes in the surface, attached to a leather strap that fitted over the head. "Perhaps I have too much time on my hands but I had to create something to stop my subjects protesting."

Before Abigail had a chance to move Morbridge had reached her side. Clutching her thin hair he wrenched her head back, strapping the monstrosity about her, the pointed prongs forced past her lips, digging sharply into her tongue.

He leant forward imposingly, his heated breath warming the tears that were beginning to slip from her limpid eyes.

"Speak and taste blood, little lovely. Any attempt and that point will penetrate." He reached around and tightened the strap roughly, pinning her tongue further and jarring her teeth. "I need concentration! Not puerile protests!"

Tears began to slide more freely down her cheeks, earning a snort of disdain.

"Crying simply worsens your condition but you are a woman so what more could I expect?" He turned from her and carried on back to the drawer, sifting through its contents cautiously. The needle he withdrew was blunted, it had been used many times before but since it still penetrated the skin it still had worth.

Abigail gave a choked sob, the salty droplets trickling into her mouth and down her throat. The prong dug in as she attempted to swallow and added a metallic taste as blood joined them.

A calloused hand gripped her neck, forcing her head to the side and a stinging pain rushed through her as the dulled point drove through skin and muscle to seek a vein.

Echoes.

White.

Silence.

Darkness.

Unfeeling eyes gazed at the barely breathing form. Lifting her lids to examine the glazed orbs beneath.

Deftly he removed the mouthpiece, casting it aside until next time and hoisted her from the seat, placing her recumbent body on the table.

The room was soon filled with the sound of metal on bone, a sickly scent of blood chasing away the musty odour.

• • •

Morbridge exhaled in exasperation as he watched the convulsions and listened to the choking. The concern was not for the woman inhaling her own blood but for the fact his experiment had not been finished.

Shaking his head he pulled the sheet over Abigail's head and waited for the body to still.

"Another one for the fire," he muttered, "but a useful specimen for dissection beforehand."

Seldom were the bodies ever claimed. Family wanted little to do with them in life or death. Who wanted to stigma of madness staining their names?

It was unfortunate only because whilst one could cut the skin to probe the organs beneath, study and analyse the ailments that blight the flesh one could not dissect the mind to reveal the mysteries. No, that had to be achieved when the specimen was alive.

He seized the limp arm roughly, wrapping the sheet more tightly about her. He didn't want to see those glassy, lifeless eyes staring at him.

Damning him.

His grip was overly tight, adding bruises that would not fade as the blood began to cool. It wouldn't matter. The skin was unimportant. His only thought was on dragging her to the lower room and ridding her of those orbs that accused him.

Chapter Twelve

Silas glanced at the bread on offer when James brought it in, giving a grimace before pushing it aside.

"As fond as I am of plant life I refuse to eat it," he said with a shudder, "at least when it grows where it should not."

James looked at the drying crust. The softer innards were dappled with green where mould had taken up residence. He shook his head.

"I can't say I blame you."

Silas sat back, idly twirling a lock of his silvery hair, giving a sigh.

"The days pass by and no one knows unless they watch the growth of fungi," he added in a singsong manner, "or hear the rocks as they crumble into the abyss of the sea."

"That's a rather morbid depiction, Mr Everett," James replied absently, watching the slender fingers nimbly braid the tress they toyed with. He repressed a snigger, causing a snort to emerge instead.

"It is rude of me to ask what it is you find so amusing?"

"I perhaps shouldn't mention it," James turned for a moment to regain his composure, continuing to speak, "but seeing that it's no wonder Morbridge labels you effeminate."

Silas gave a smirk.

"You say that like it's an insult."

"Is it not?"

"Not to me. Old Morbid can call me what he wishes." Seeing the quizzical expression, Silas continued, leaning further back in the crudely padded chair whose limbs creaked in protest. He pressed his fingertips together as he gazed at him evenly. "Some things we cannot change, my dear friend, lying is apparently a sin so lying about whom or what you are must be the greatest of all." He flicked his wrist and tossed his leg over the arm of the seat in a relaxed fashion. "Accept your lot and find your path, that it the challenge for every man, yourself included."

"I believe I have already found my path in life, I need look no further," James retorted but his voice was weak, uncertainty lacing it. He swallowed, is eyes shifting to the barred windows. "And if I haven't then I suppose it will reveal itself."

Silas continued as if he had not heard the reply, rocking the chair on its back legs. Or perhaps he had heard and was simply disregarding it.

"You cannot change your past either but you can create your future if you seize that chance."

James nodded nonchalantly as he turned for the door, gripping the handle more tightly than normal.

"I'll do that," he indicated in the direction of the bread, swiftly moving the subject. "I'll have to leave that. They'll be furious if I take it back."

"Furious with others. I'm no charity case, I pay my way, or my partner does," Silas said with a proud toss of his head "but do as you wish. I would not want to cause much trouble."

"Good, because I'm the one who'll get it," James muttered as he slipped from the room "they don't need an excuse either."

"Since I'm doing you a good turn you could do me one," he heard Silas add. He held the door ajar so just a sliver of the room remained and he could hear. "You can be a dear and see if there are any letters. Everyone else is that lax they'd be there for years."

Despite the man being unable to see him James nodded his agreement, letting the heavy door close with a loud click.

He took the pencil that he had left outside on the ledge; it was unwise to even take a blunt object such as that inside. Even though he was comfortable enough in the feeling that Silas wasn't one to take such an action as gouging an eye out.

Or maybe that was just a lull before a storm? One could never tell.

He jotted down a note to check the office once his break was finished, adding a mental addition to attempt speaking again to Marianne. He could still hear the charming, girlish voice that never left her lips. It intrigued him to hear more, to know more of the silent woman with such hidden talents.

Making his way back up the dingy stairwell he smiled to himself, a smile that made his eyes shine as it reached them. A smile that lasted until he saw his door was ajar.

"For goodness sake," he muttered as he approached "do I get no privacy?"

He expected a mess when he entered. To see his drawers pulled open and item scattered over the rumpled blanket on the bed but to his surprise nothing seemed touched. Everything was as it was when he had left that morning.

Except for a folded paper that had been placed at his bedside. That hadn't been there that morning.

He reached for it, peeling back the corner to peek at the writing beneath, smelling a faint scent of flowers as he did so. When he saw the childish scrawl within it he cast it away hurriedly.

The image of the picture came to mind and he didn't want to see it, however curious he was.

Returning to the bed he sat slowly, his gaze not leaving the paper that fluttered down to the floor even as his body continued and he soon lay on his back.

He forced his eyes to closer, trying to sink into an uneasy doze to clear his head.

As the lucidity of dreams overtook him James felt a warm hand envelop his own.

'James?' A female voice whispered urgently yet soothingly *'James, please wake, look at me. See me!'*

Fear kept his eyes closed but he felt sorrow flood his heart and could almost feel the tears he sensed filled the speaker's eyes.

"Marianne?" he mumbled, knowing only one woman with a voice so sweet. "You shouldn't be here."

There was a choked sob.

'No James...'

The voice and footsteps faded away.

Chapter Thirteen

The basement was a cesspool of gore.

Blood splatters decorated a once clean wall. Shreds of decomposing tissue and fetid bodily fluid formed a sticky paste on the floor.

Even rats, who emerged to seize a loose piece of flesh, hurried away shortly after, the stench cleaving to their sensitive nostrils.

Another metal table stood on rusted legs, remnants of the last butchered occupant still clinging to its surface.

The rest of them had been consumed by the fire, along with other unfortunates.

Morbridge hauled the light body down the spiralling stairway, the action made hard because of the dark rather than weight.

Dropping her on the concrete he took a breath, placing his hands on his hips.

His clothing resembled that of a careless butcher. The white stained with drying crimson and emitted a pungent odour.

Shrugging his shoulders he let the gown slide from them, heedlessly tossing it into the corner with the others waiting to be washed.

The bodies weren't kept well, he had no real areas to store them but since they did not lie for long before study the basement seemed the best place. It was cool and dark and out of the way. This did not halt the decomposition but it slowed it slightly, the best one could ask for.

The dark eyes remained on the form beneath the fabric, a red stain seeping through the snow white sheet where the injuries still exuded blood.

"Such a waste," he muttered in malcontent. "A fine form but your body and mind were weak. To have drowned you like an unwanted orphan would have been fairer on us all."

She would at least offer surgical practice and a further look into the organs that caused her ills. He nudged her body into the colder corner, turning to leave. As he reached the base of the steps he paused, glancing back as if something had caught his attention.

A rat scurried from the shadows, its pink nose sniffing as it picked up the scent of fresh blood. A dark glaze formed in the doctor's eyes, darker than the beady orbs of the rodent.

Moving over swiftly, he brought his heel down upon the creatures' skull, smiling as he heard the snap of bone and crunch of flesh.

He wasn't going to use half-eaten corpses again.

• • •

James had risen early having given up on trying to rest. The voice and strange sounds had disturbed his dreams, keeping him in a state of neither sleep nor wakefulness, it left him with the feeling his head was full of fog.

He hoped by rising and keeping himself occupied until his shift started he could relieve that. And since he had promised Silas to check the post it seemed like an ideal time. The lack of alertness could be hazardous.

He met no one on his way to the office. The corridors were as quiet and still as a tomb with not even the sound of mice scurrying in the walls to alleviate it.

As normal the room was in disarray. A hemp sack containing letters from months, maybe years ago sat limply in the corner, surrounded by dust and scattered papers that were no longer needed. Originally it had probably been a workplace for someone but now it seemed it was used as a dumping ground for waste.

James wrinkled his nose as he eased the sack open, pulling the letters out between two fingers, one by one. The ink faded on the envelopes and most were unreadable.

"Thank the Gods we get little post," he muttered as he dropped them aside, "I dread to think of the chaos."

But a feeling of sadness coupled with that thought, sadness that so many were simply forgotten here, erased from the memory of their loved ones, simply because their minds had become strained.

After several more were set aside James finally found two that were legible. The crumpling indicated they had sat for some time. Silas's name was faded but it was clear enough and James pushed it into his pocket.

The other he was not sure about, feeling the cold chill in his stomach as he read his own name. Why would it be in a pile with those of the patients?

Part of him wanted to throw it back, forget he had seen it but he knew all too well it would prey on his mind should he do that.

With a sigh of exasperation, he shoved it into his pocket. Perhaps if he kept it with him unopened then that would be enough.

• • •

Silas didn't appear to have moved, shifting in his seat only when James entered.

James said nothing, silently holding out the letter. Silas paused, looking as if he was going to offer his normal sarcasm but decided against it, taking the note in silence.

He flicked it open, placidly scanning the words. James watched as his brow furrowed in confusion, the expression soon turning to fury, brightening his already intense eyes.

"Damn them!" Silas erupted, hurling the letter in a tight ball across the room; it bounced several times before settled in the corner. "Toy with my emotions and then rip them apart!" He brought his fist down on the table, so hard a crack appeared on the glossy surface. "Thank the Gods I am in here already, I'd strangle them!"

James leapt back, his hand on the door but frozen in place. He had never been witness to a flare of the others temper, fiery enough to strike fear into a devil itself.

"He may not be you," Silas cited coldly. "Of course he's not bloody me!"

He sat down heavily, giving a long sigh as if exhaling the anger from his body, head in his hands.

"God damn it." Silas slowly looked up "let this be a lesson to you, boy, never give your heart to anyone, they always shatter it in the end in one way or another," he shook his head "I refused to speak their name to save them the indignity of even being known here. Now I shall not speak it in the hope of abolishing the very memory."

He gestured towards the paper with a snort of irritation.

"Take it and burn it, it warrants no response and judging by the date it is too late anyway."

James stooped to pick up the discarded note that lay nearby; it fell open as he took hold of it, allowing him to reach the neat script.

I loved you dearly when your mind was straight but I can no longer wait on an impossible dream.

You would approve of my new partner; he is not you but is as caring as you once were.

He flinched at the underlying tone, that they no longer cared and their heart had turned from the one they had once gifted it to.

P.S. Your comfort will not be taken; I owe you that at least.

James took another glance at Silas who had slumped motionlessly at his desk. His eyes and thoughts lost in a world far beyond that which he currently inhabited.

The meaningless objet d'art was all that were left and he doubted the man would care whether it remained or not.

Once that had been a symbol that there was at least one person who cared but now they were a painful reminder of someone's betrayal.

The overwhelming urge was to remain. To offer what limited comfort he could but the flair of temper had been a clear warning and his sudden slump an indication he would resent his presence.

He nodded towards the unhappy figure and slipped from the room, shutting the door as quietly as he was able.

Robotically he headed down the eerily silent corridors and out into the courtyard, slowly tearing the unwanted letter, letting the wind carry it up and away like petals blown from a blossom tree.

He stood listening to the mighty roar of the tides outside the walls, sounding as though Leviathan himself stirred beneath; the island itself seemed to tremble. As if the ocean fed on the turbulence that rocked the skies.

Or maybe it was just his imagination again.

It was clammy out. The air mingled with the briny spray and droplets of rain which clung to his pale skin.

James knew this wasn't helpful but surrounding himself with the walls of breezy darkness was preferable to being entombed by those of stone and sorrow.

He watched at the final pieces floated away. People feared asylums, afraid to 'catch' the dreaded madness as if it was transmitted simply by being in another's presence. Or perhaps even by holding a letter sent by one of their unfortunate loved ones.

It was a falsehood. Yet at that moment when he looked at the running ink of the one addressed to him he couldn't help but wonder.

A sudden gush of water nearby caused him to jolt to his senses. Looking down a river of stained fluid trickled across the cobbles, emptied from a rusting bucket.

Morbridge glanced over; making no sign he was going to say anything. Placing the pail down he removed a handkerchief, wrinkling his nose as he wiped the residue from his fingers.

"Don't others normally clean?" James could have kicked himself, the question sounded stupid and the doctor was not one to start conversation with but the need to hear a voice in the black overwhelmed him. "Why not summon them?"

"Because there was no call to. And it reduces any alarm."

Alarm?

Looking down again James saw the scraps of skin and tissue sticking to the stone. A rush of revulsion flowed through him, faster and stronger than the bloody water at his feet.

"Problem?"

James's eye rose to meet the sneer of the doctor, idly stroking the bloody handle of the bucket. He swallowed and looked away.

"No. I'm most certainly not the one with a problem," he ran his fingers through his hair, scattering the rain that clung to the blonde strands. He crumpled the letter and tossed it down, the blood saturating into the paper. "Much to be said for the doctors being worse than those they claim to treat."

He stalked away without another glance, Morbridge's low chuckle reverberating in his ears. The door slammed after him, blocking the offensive sound.

'To penetrate your future is his greatest crime.'

The voice appeared in his mind, causing an ache to throb through his temples. The voice was not that of Marianne, he was certain.

But maybe she would know what was causing it, after all that was her skill and if another possessed it, then perhaps she would sense it.

• • •

It was not hard to find a task that would allow him access to the female section. None of the men liked interfacing with the sour matron and often patient records and information was left until there was no other option.

James was no exception. The thin and bitter woman was no joy to speak with but to see Marianne he needed to do so.

However the matron was a woman of few words and once she had received the wrongly delivered letters she muttered a few curse words about the incompetence of the others and abruptly gestured for him to leave.

He hesitated for a few moments once he left her spruce office, listening to the rustle of papers to satisfy himself that she was not going to emerge for some time.

Continuing down the gloomy corridor he ignored the unhappy sounds from the other patients, most shackled and fearful in the corners of their rooms.

It was hard. To listen to such woe and not react, the soft sobs that emanated from within, that seemed to follow him.

Marianne was sat on her bed, her knees drawn to her chest as still as a statue. Her eyes rose as the door jangled, lighting up to see the figure that entered.

"Hello again," James gave a warm smile towards her. "How have you been?"

Marianne nodded slowly, her eyes beaming for her, her voice filling his senses like a sweet perfume.

"I've been dreaming, imagining a world of fragile beauty."

Forgetting his own question for a moment James looked curious, silently encouraging her to continue.

"I dream of field of golden daffodils that waltz in the wind, I think of dancing through them and with them."

The voice ceased and her brow furrowed into a frown. Silence fell and James took it to mean she had finished, upset merely by the thought of what she could never hope to see.

"A pretty vision, I hope one day that you will be able to feel that, you don't belong in this place, a lot of you don't." He sighed and looked at the cold stone floor, continuing cautiously, "Marianne, does anyone else have your skill? To talk without speaking?"

The answer was not to come. Marianne's speech resumed as if she had never paused, a silvery tear glittering in her eye.

"Not beautiful...I hear them cry, hear them wail as my feet touch them, crush them. They live, wretched as their existence is. They are alive like us and like me they are believed to feel naught. Trapped in a garden made of glass, fearful of shattering at any moment." Her face fell and her eyes clouded as she drifted away, "Oh how they cry, just like a baby."

James's lips moved but no sound would emerge, unable to move or raise his voice to give any comfort. Even if it was a simple superficial comment it could have offered some solace.

Marianne rocked herself robotically, cradling an invisible babe in her arms before her head dropped forward and her body wilted.

"No. No one else. I am alone. I am always alone with only the ghosts of memories to haunt me."

James swallowed, inching forward and watching his shadow stretch out as it mirrored his movements.

He rested a hand on her thin shoulder, squeezing her collarbone.

She was lost to him and made no sign of even feeling his touch or noting his presence anymore.

James knew there was little point in staying, curious as he was about the reaction, about her dreams.

He slipped from the room as silently as he was able; every sound seemed heightened in this place. He took a final look back at the closed door, hoping to hear some noise from the room but there was none.

Just the sound of the wind outside.

Chapter Fourteen

James saw no one as he returned to his room but could not shake the feeling that his every movement was being watched by some unseen eye.

He sighed and shook his head. Sheer paranoia, this place had a talent of making one feel that way in every waking moment. It felt like this much of the time but...somehow today felt worse.

The hope diminished as the door screeched open, revealing the blooded note fastened to the wall, still unopened.

He froze the doorway, pushing his fringe back to prove to himself that his uncovered eye was not deceiving him.

It wasn't.

His lips moved but no sound emerged as he edged closer, knocking his hip sharply on the open drawer as he did so.

He couldn't even swear as the sting travelled through the bone.

"This is ridiculous," James managed to stutter, forcing the words from his throat simply to break the ominous silence. "This is a pathetic joke and it isn't going to work!"

He tore the paper down and torn it in two, trying not the glance at the scrawled writing that lay within, throwing it violently into the corner.

Giving a long and lethargic sigh he sat down on the bed, rubbing his temples before looking over to the open drawer, the contents clearly disordered.

He reached to shut it, pausing when he noticed the ornate knife he kept was missing. A chill of unease rippled through him as he shifted the already untidy items aside in the hope it was simply hidden underneath the papers.

He bit his lip. Anything such as that was forbidden despite the knowledge most of the wardens here claimed amongst them to have something of the like. But it wasn't the type of item to leave lying about or to lose. The excuse it was simply sentimental would not hold.

"Calm it," he whispered aloud to himself, taking a breath to still his increased heart beat, "it will turn up. There is nothing to worry about, it cannot be far. It is a pathetic joke that is going too far."

The words seemed hollow and did little to soothe his nerves. He cursed himself for being highly strung; he should have overcome that by now.

He slammed the drawer shut, flopping back onto the bed, closing his eyes to quell the headache that was beginning to throb through his sinuses.

• • •

Strange lights flickered, emitting an odd humming sound as if a swarm of insects panicked frantically within them.

There was so much white.

Too much white.

White walls, white bedding.

Not again.

James sat up, sickness rolling within his body. He clutched his stomach, feeling as if a thousand needles were piercing his gastric lining.

Why was this happening?

It had to be stress. An irrational illusion that would be banished as his mind calmed down. *When* his mind calmed down, that alone seemed impossible.

The floor was cold as he inched forward and placed his feet down. The pull of curiosity pulled him on, dulling the fear. He needed to know what this was, *why* this was.

Reaching the door he looked down a sickly green corridor, a bitter chemical scent burning his nose, the smell reminded him of the pungent fluids they used to mop away the accumulated filth when they deigned to clean a vacant room.

But that only masked a smell. This was pure.

His neck ached as he turned his head to look around. This was wrong, all wrong.

The lights hanging above and those glowing yellow behind cloudy patches in the wall hurt his head, sending throbbing aches behind his eyes as they strained against it to see properly. But everything seemed hazy.

There was a sound from somewhere nearby, the soft scuff of footfalls.

James fled. He didn't want to see anymore of this purgatory.

He flung himself back down onto the strange bed, burying his head in the pillow, counting slowly in his head.

Once again as he opened his eyes the room had shifted, returning to the familiar bleak surroundings. He lay still for several moments, trembling.

After a few uncomfortable moments he slowly sat up. Normally he liked being alone but for some reason the emptiness felt wrong, eerie and unnatural. He didn't want to seek the other warders; they were of no use and Silas would no doubt still be brooding.

That left only Marianne, even silent and distant she was company. It was a risk but one he was willing to take just to break the monotony and the stillness. To leave the ominous weight that bore down behind him.

Chapter Fifteen

"I was dreaming again, dreaming in my waking hours."

Marianne's 'voice' met James as soon as he reached her door, as if she knew who stood behind it despite the iron between them.

"I saw great figures, rising through a jagged roof, as if they are trying to escape," she rocked herself idly side to side as the warden entered. "A woman, grown from a girl in pieces at her feet, frozen in a run, her hair still flowing behind, a fragile marble. At her feet there is a boy, he cannot grow and is unable to stand tall, simply cowering to hide from a shrouded figure."

James nodded, only half listening. He knew it was another cryptic ramble about herself and the loss of the child.

"They are so still," she continued in a sorrowful tone, "perhaps they shall crumble into happy rubble together with the great walls that confine them or, like us, perhaps they are simply trapped in a world beyond their control?"

"Do you have these dreams often?" James queried, speaking aloud whilst he was in her presence. He had a headache from his own dreams and it seemed more sensible. He glanced away. "Lucid dreaming seems common here."

Marianne looked up, tilting her head as her eyes sparkled in the dim light. She seemed to be looking right through him, searching.

"Dreams are a gate to a new world," she answered smoothly, a smile tweaking her pink lips. "Not always a good world but you can learn from them nonetheless. Sometimes they contain signs and omens that one should heed, revealing trapped memories that need release."

As if hypnotised James moved toward her and cupped her cold

cheek sympathetically with a warming hand. Clearly he didn't understand or didn't believe her words, dreams were simply ones imagination working whilst one was lost in slumber.

Her gentle eyes lifted to meet his. Silence settled between them.

The crash of metal startled James back to reality, snatching his hand back swiftly and looking over his shoulder in alarm.

A flush appeared on his cheeks as he felt the cool tingle of her lingering on his fingertips.

"I have to go," he said quietly, giving a tense flutter of his lips, an attempted smile. "If I'm caught here I'll be in serious trouble."

She nodded. "Speak to me and I shall hear. It gets easier the more you listen, the more you try."

"I will, I promise."

James touched her hand briefly before retreating swiftly from the room. Rather than feeling better he felt even more flustered.

Despite his caution his door slammed shut behind him, muffling the sound of hurried footsteps.

He didn't want to go back to his room but other than facing the contempt of the others he had little option.

That choice was soon snatched from him as he passed by the entrance of the dining hall and caught sight of a fellow warder standing outside, still as stone until he neared, as if he had only been activated by the other's presence.

"Good timing. You can go downstairs instead of me," the older male said curtly, his eyes cold and disinterested in any answer. "It isn't worth wasting my energy to put a few ticks on paper. You're younger and have more to spare."

"What?" James shook his head vigorously, pausing to adjust his fringe which flicked out of place. "I've done my shift, do your own damn job!"

The man glared at him. "Call it a favour, Grey. If you do that I won't tell Morbridge I think you're coming unhinged."

James's eyes narrowed.

"I may be thinking over a lot but I am most certainly not unhinged! Whatever mind I lost then I lost it a long while back and I am not planning on losing anything else!"

"Does that matter? Half the imbeciles here say that when they arrive and keep it up even when they're rolling about in their own filth. No one believes them and no one would believe you either."

The words were blunt and matter of fact. The folded arms adding to the effect.

James's eyes narrowed darkly and he took a breath, biting the inside of his cheek to calm the rising temper that he could not afford to lose.

"Fine. But why do I feel that if I ever need a favour then there's no point in asking you?"

The man snorted. Dignifying a foolish question with an obvious answer seemed pointless. He ambled away, muttering under his breath, a few words reaching James's ears, causing him to arch an eyebrow. Such language!

Giving a long and exasperated sigh he turned on his heel abruptly, heading towards the stairs to the basement. There was no use in putting things off, one look and he was done. But halfway down the tenebrous steps he froze, remembering that low, malicious voice.

Even the thought of it was enough to make him shudder.

'Please come back...'

His eyes widened as the voice whispered about him, the sorrowful female voice that refused to leave him be.

He felt torn. He didn't want to continue down to the beast's lair but nor did he want to turn and face whatever was behind.

If anything.

And if nothing was there it surely only cemented the others words that he was losing himself.

Reluctantly and with shivers running down his spine James looked over his shoulder. Only to see nothing at all.

He wasn't certain if this was a relief or not. Part of him hoped to see something, just to prove he wasn't going mad. But when he thought of it without another to witness that sort of proof would not hold much weight.

"Good grief, pull yourself together man!" James cursed to

himself, striding boldly down the stairs, filling the silence with the sound of loud footfalls.

The bold pace tapered off as he reached the bottom and his eyes saw the bolted door when they adjusted to the gloom.

The recollection of his last encounter came rushing back. The strange aura that hovered like a lingering spirit about the room and the feel of him watching even though his eyes were covered.

"One look," James muttered, "one look and I leave. No need to remain any longer unless something urgent is required."

Simple.

He tossed his head and left the last step but his pace remained slow, fearful of making any sound that would let Nathaniel know of his presence.

But those blind to the world, natural or not, had sharp hearing.

A low chuckle emanated from within the locked room, echoing about him.

"Because of their parents the children pay, strangled by their loving tourniquet."

The urge to simply turn, taking the words as a validation that the man was alright. He was alive anyway.

But although most others would have done just that it would be negligent and if something did happen to go wrong then the blame would be squarely at his feet. As abhorrent as the man was he couldn't allow laxness in duty.

Taking a breath of the fetid air he moved onward and approached the heavy door, pausing for a brief moment before sliding the hatch back with a loud click.

Nathaniel was still as he always has. The only movement was a slight twitch of his fingers as he flexed them occasionally.

"So we meet again, the friend of the mute, the friend of the madman," Nathaniel breathed maliciously, "and yet I sense you are as bemused as ever, your soul dying even as you stand there."

"My soul is perfectly fine, thank you," James answered resolutely. "It is a shame I cannot say the same about your own."

"Black as a night without stars or moon," Nathaniel almost purred almost proudly, "and if light appears than it is soon quashed."

James wrinkled his nose and snapped the hatch shut, pausing as he heard more whispered words, straining his ears to hear through the door.

'Who will be incriminated now?'

The voice being so soft, the words almost a hiss, it was nigh-on impossible to be certain if that was the statement he heard.

"Perhaps I am dreaming whilst still awake," James muttered as he turned resignedly. "Marianne can surely not be the only one to do that."

But Marianne found beauty amongst the ugliness in her dreams. He saw only darkness.

Hastily he mounted the stairs which seemed so much longer than they had when he descended a few moments ago.

• • •

Silas was still brooding when he heard soft footsteps that paused behind the door. He gave a sigh and turned to look over his shoulder, his glossy hair falling in a cascade down his back.

"I'm sufficiently calm that you're not in danger of a chair launched at your head," Silas said in a loud enough voice to carry, "so don't dally if you wish to speak, even though the hour groweth late."

The chair swivelled around as the door was gingerly eased open.

"Silas..."

"Ah! We are back on first name terms! How stupendous!" Silas pressed his hands together as if silently applauding.

James gave a blink of a smile.

"Well I cannot ever remember us being so but I shall take your word for it. All things considered it's fair I suppose."

"You do that, I know best," his lazy eyes sparkled, resuming the knowing exuberance "from apothecary to zephyr. And considering you all seem oblivious to a comforting Earl Grey I suppose your company will suffice."

"I'd give you my ration but..."

"Dishwater," Silas finished with a knowing smirk "and of course who know what a person such as I would do with tepid water, hmm?"

James chuckled.

"Third degree burns no doubt, but you'd also have to see Morbridge or the nurse."

Silas shuddered.

"I'd rather not see Old Morbid or the skinny creature that masquerades as a nurse." He arched an indignant eyebrow at the badly suppressed snort which morphed into a cough in an attempt to cover it. "And that is amusing how?"

"My apologies, I just think it's rather a fitting pet name," James said as he composed himself, leaning back against the door in order to keep a sharp ear out for any approach.

"A satirical term of endearment would be my description but call it what you wish," Silas flung his legs onto the desk and examined his nails, "but I don't think you came simply for idle chitchat did you? I don't mind but I sense more pressing issues."

James muttered something under his breath.

Silas cocked his head and looked at him intently, rocking back and forth in his chair.

"Why is Marianne really here?" James asked breathily as if he was speaking and sighing in tandem. "For surely being mute is no reason to be confined? And I am certain she is no killer."

"That isn't your true question, I can tell," Silas replied smoothly, lacing his fingers, "but I shall humour you, Marianne was brought after what was most likely a forced miscarriage. She was not born a mute but her voice was silenced at eleven. When she birthed her own brother."

A sickening silence fell as James digested the foul words, the implication of which took a short moment to register.

Birthing her own brother.

The image of a classroom was suddenly envisioned. The scenery vague but the blurred visage of an unhappy girl, sat trying to hide away in the corner, was the focal point. He shook his head, trying to rid himself of it, he didn't understand these visions and they perturbed him.

"Try not to dwell upon it," Silas advised as he gazed at him. "It turns the stomach and stirs the temper."

James's gaze moved to the grubby floor. The advice was easier said than done, the idea was foul and almost impossible to erase.

"Maybe we ought to move on?" Silas suggested as he watched the others expression. "Pull your thoughts from such things?"

"Perhaps, although I doubt it will leave now the seed is sowed." He gave a long sigh and moved from the door, none could walk so softly that their feet made no sound here, sitting rather rigidly on the bed.

Silas made a small murmur of agreement but nothing more, waiting for the man to continue speaking whilst continuing to rock in his chair.

Silence. Eventually another long sigh.

"It is this place," he said quietly. "It feels wrong, more than it has done in the past. Although I'll be honest and say I hardly remember the past. As if I have simply existed here for all time. I find myself wanting to run from these doors and return to the mainland."

"Do not crave the rose if you cannot bear its thorns, James. They are what you must edge your way through, acting rashly increases the injury."

James decided to the shift the subject, not comfortable with speaking of himself or his flights of fancy. Talking could help but he resented doing so, at least with someone who had his own issues. It didn't seem right or fair.

He fidgeted on a lump in the mattress, causing the springs to squeak like startled mice.

"What were you, Silas?"

Silas blinked, his eyes seeming more luminous in the gloom with only a sliver of light entering inside.

"An odd question with an obvious answer I would think. I was a man, unfortunately, same as I am now."

"No, I meant your occupation, before you came here."

"Oh, I see. I worked the graveyards, simple work of keeping them tidy, stop them falling into disrepair. Fascinating in a way, especially when you look at the diversity of humans beneath the earth, proves in the end we are all the same and end the same. Ashes to ashes, dust to dust." He gave an unnerving, rather macabre smile, recalling the artistry of death before adding hastily, "And I assure you that my record does not state I had alternative uses for corpses. The very idea is repulsive."

"Glad to hear it," James said quietly. "We already have one atrocity below I have to deal with, I don't think I could endure another."

"No."

Once again silence rolled over them like the incoming tide. Finally Silas spoke, gazing at James solemnly.

"You still haven't really covered the reason for your visit, my friend, and I fear you are not going to. But understand that keeping thoughts locked away can be detrimental."

James nodded.

"Dreams again," he said with reticence, his voice lowered. "The same one as before which is what confused me. How is it possible I can dream about the same place, an identical place, two nights consecutively?"

Silas pursed his lips.

"I'm not entirely sure. I can imagine one dreams of the same places, I've dreamt of places that I am certain I have before, nothing that exists in real life but I feel I have been there in the land of sleep." He smirked. "Perhaps you are under a curse?"

"Certainly feels as if I am." James got up to pace the room, feeling the others eyes watch him, bright and vibrant as though laughing. "Another thing is I seem to find things odd that are clearly commonplace. One of the others was rambling earlier and said something, the word is just deemed a colour but I found the connotation offensive."

"Ah, you mean ni…"

"Yes."

He didn't want to explain more, fearing repercussion even though Silas seemed completely accepting, taking it all seriously in his detached manner as though it was as normal as breathing. He flicked his wrist and turned away, resuming his habit of twirling his silvery hair.

Before James could speak again the sound of muffled voices,

mingled with the sound of footsteps pulled his attention back to the door.

The voices were light, feminine but no women walked this way, forbidden to leave the female wards unless given express permission.

He looked to Silas who shifted his shoulders in a parody of a shrug.

The little colour he had drained from his face. Giving a small nod towards him James hastened to the door, opening enough to slip through without allowing any view of the corridor beyond.

Chapter Sixteen

The corridor seemed brighter than normal. Cleaner and as if bathed in glorious rays of sun, the likes of which never penetrated the steely building.

James's temples throbbed; his skull feeling as though it was pulsating in pain as he stepped forward into the unusual lustre.

He felt blindly for the door behind him to pull it shut, the soft click considerably muted when he thought of the harsh clang of iron he was used to.

The voices echoed further down the passage and around the sharp corner. Whoever spoke sounded so cheerful, an emotion few were used to hearing.

It was a happy noise but one that was completely alien to the sprawling building and consequently evoked fear rather than pleasure.

His feet felt as though leaden weights were attached to the soles, each step a draining effort. As he moved forward his nervousness grew, the compulsion to stop making it feel as though he were wading through tar.

His heart pulsating so rapidly it was almost a droning hum.

He rounded the corner painfully; his fingers taut and arthritic clutched the wall as coldness washed over him like a rising tide, his body beginning to shake violently.

The voices ceased.

The sound of rushing feet was the last thing he heard before sinking into blackness.

When he awoke he was back in his room again as if nothing had happened and no time had passed.

All was well with the world again.

James lay still, toying with the corner of the flocked blanket as he regained himself. Slowly he rolled himself over to the face the wall, raking his fingers through the asymmetrical fringe, finding the dull, chipped stone a far better view than the cracked ceiling.

There was a soft rustling outside as a frigid rain waltzed wildly with sleet in the air and coerced the trees to move with them.

Muscles he didn't know he had ached, stiff from either the fall or spasms, if indeed they had occurred. It may well have been yet another horrific trick of his mind.

"Pull yourself together; you're a man not a mouse!" James cursed himself furiously. "Just because you're around insanity all day does not mean it is catching. You're simply allowing your mind to run amok!"

He struggled into a sitting position, resting his head in his hands while he allowed it to catch up and his vision to settle.

"Stupid!" He rose unsteadily to his feet and moved to the barred window to gaze onto the dolorous surroundings, droplets falling like heavens tears down to the earth below. "Nothing ails you! Nightmares brought upon by sheer insipience!"

Taking a harsh breath, he strode to the door and flung it open, immediately hit with the freezing air. The building itself seeming colder than the freezing tides that wore the island day in and day out.

Turning to his left he met the scornful eyes of another warden. His heart jolted into his throat. Seldom did anyone come up this way anymore.

Time seemed to freeze for a moment as the pair acknowledged each other, the bulkier male seeming almost statue like until he gave a slow blink of his unpleasant eyes and took in the sight of his dishevelled colleague.

The man's fingers seemed distended like the talons of a bird, gnarled and worked as they toyed with a pencil in his hand.

With a scornful sniff he turned to leave, the sound making it clear what he thought.

"Do not shun me!"

"I can do nothing but shun you, why do I need to concern myself with another imbecile, diseased and dangerous? Or just like one of those rotten darkies who taint our sights?"

Despite the fact they had never been close James still felt the tug of pain, of abandonment. Friend or not there still seemed to be an unwritten rule of support but it seemed he was exempt from it.

His eyes shifted as a glow emanated from the darkness, unseen by the other. He continued walking towards the stairway even as the visage of the mournful female appeared.

He walked right through her.

James found his feet rooted to the spot, unable to move as glided forward, her hand outstretched to brush his face.

Her eyes like polished emeralds in a sea of snow. He couldn't count how many shades of green were concentrated in those vibrant irises.

'Please, I know you see me, hear me,' she begged, a tear beginning to fall. *'Fight on. I'm here, I'll never leave you.'*

Yanking away James darted back clumsily, his back connecting sharply with the railings behind him.

"Leave me be spirit!" He ejected towards the translucent shade, his body and voice quaking "or tell me what you want of me!"

He wasn't sure she could hear him. It felt as if a world divided them and her expression remained fixed, gazing at him with eyes that had seen both lives and dreams broken.

One again her hand extended, reaching out towards his own even though it was now far from her grasp.

Intense nausea blended with fear churned in his stomach. Mingled whispers drifted around him.

From her?

From Marianne?

Or just from inside of him?

'You don't belong here.'

He didn't know who, if anyone spoke. Not anymore as he felt himself being shrouded in a mist of bright, white lights.

Blinding and disorientating.

He didn't feel an impact or any pain as he fell, crashing to the ground. In fact, he felt comfortable, or he would if it were not for the light.

Reaching out he felt for something, *anything*, to give him some idea of where he was.

Considering where he fell, he expected to feel metal or the stone floor. He certainly didn't expect to feel thin air and a drop as if he lay on a soft but dangerous precipice. He continued to shift his hand cautiously, searching for anything tangible.

After a time his fingers brushed against something cold and hard. The smoothness indicated wood. A table?

There was something on it whatever it was.

His digits clasped what felt like a jar, turning his aching neck to see a flash of brown in the blinding whiteness.

He clutched it tightly, his knuckles becoming as white as the room he lay in.

This felt like a bad dream but he could clearly feel the jar in his hand, feel his tendons tightening as he held it.

Clamping his eyes shut almost as firmly he slowly counted in his head, praying that when he reached the number ten that this would all vanish once again.

That he would open his eyes to the hateful scenery he loathed and be glad of it.

One, two, three...

As the numbers grew higher the surface beneath him hardened like setting clay and the blinding light that penetrated his eyelids began to dull.

His heart skipped a beat as he felt the surface beneath him sink as if someone perched nearby, a suspicion that was confirmed as he felt warmer as heat sank and spread through the thin mattress.

"I have not seen such a material as that," a familiar voice sounded, "nor such medication. May I ask where you obtained it?"

James's eyes snapped open, meeting the solemn gaze of Silas sat on the end of the bed, obscuring his vision of the door and where he had fell. He motioned to the jar still clutched in his hand.

"S-Silas? How did you...?"

Silas raised a hand. "Time for idle curiosities later," he

interrupted impatiently, twiddling his lengthy fingers, "but indulge mine, will you?"

James sighed, his head had started to throb and he hadn't the energy to argue. Had Silas answered his query he probably would not have been able to process the information anyway.

He looked at the jar, turning it over in shaking hands, unable to properly read the faded label stuck on the surface. Inside thin syrup splashed about, forming hard little bubbles upon the surface.

"I'm not sure. I think Morbridge keeps newer drugs; perhaps he decided I needed them? Fainting on the job is hardly something one can ignore as a physician."

Silas arched an eyebrow.

"I see." His tone could not conceal the doubt he held. "Well, I would be wary of taking anything that charlatan promotes as remedy but perhaps I am too rash to judge? He may actually have curative items that he simply does not see fit to use."

He held out a hand expectantly. Without a second thought James handed it over, watching as the vibrant eyes looked it over.

James's explanation did not shed light on the construction of the bottle but that matter seemed so paltry he was not about to push it.

He also felt the answer was somewhat too vague but it was not for him to cast judgement upon.

"Are you going to enlighten me to how you got out?" James's voice broke the short silence "or am I going to have to accept I am losing my own mind and that you may just be another trick of my imagination?"

"The latter theory, whilst understandable, isn't something you need to worry about," Silas replied calmly "but as for how I can to be here I shall put it as simply as I am able. Marianne states there are ways beyond words, I shall state that there are ways beyond locks."

"Well that explains a lot," James muttered sarcastically "always a goldmine of answers, aren't you?"

Silas gave a rumbling chuckle and shook his head slowly from side to side, his hair falling forward in wispy waves.

He pushed it back.

"Such mockery! I think my explanation was fitting enough!" He shifted back to sit in a more comfortable position, folding his arms "I always said no one takes me seriously and when I deign to be serious I'm taken less seriously!"

James gave a faint smile at the pout that appeared on the others face. It was hard to decipher what age Silas was, whilst his hair was as grey as the oldest human his skin and certainly his heart was childlike.

Flawless if one was to ignore the few lines beneath the soulful eyes.

"I am doomed to be a jester, added to the likes of Yorick and Rigoletto," Silas added with zeal, "yet unlike their good selves I am also doomed to be erased from history!"

The soft pad of catlike footsteps stopped any reply leaving James's lips, his gaze moving nervously towards the door where the slim crack gave a scant view of who approached. But whoever it has stood back and only a flit of white grace appeared for a brief moment before the door eased open.

He relaxed to see Marianne's enigmatic smile, her pretty face a pleasant view after the darkness he felt he had faced and still faced.

'There are ways beyond doors,' her voice filled his mind as she shared a knowing look with Silas who responded with a roll of his eyes.

"So I have heard," James responded, amusement lacing his voice "not that I understand it. However, I shall not quibble over it, your company is appreciated greatly."

Marianne's eyes appeared to beam in the dimness before she drifted to the window, looking out with fascination at the thickset trees beyond the bars, sniffing the cold but fresh air, devoid of the scent of urine or filthy bodies.

The joy in her eyes brought a smile of content to James's lips, an expression not unnoticed by Silas who smirked to himself.

The human heart was so predictable.

James could not deny Marianne looked beautiful when the smile brightened her eyes, showing the handsomeness that had been slowly drained over the years, sapped away to join the woe that resided within the stones.

"It isn't the finest view but it gives some colour to the drabbed," James said quietly, scuffing his foot on the floor "seems a shame to put blinds or curtains to shut it out."

"Life should not be taken from ones sight," Marianne answered "life is beautiful in any form; even the darkest can have some light."

When James considered the black souls that disguised themselves as workers and those who dwelled in the lower regions it was a hard thing to see. Deep down he knew the words were right but seeing it was like holding a dying candle in the gloom to light one's way.

Almost impossible.

Sensing disconcertion Marianne moved over, her slim hand caressing his cheek.

"I will stay with you if you wish," she smiled kindly, her eyes the image of a loving friend, "none will know."

"Well *I* will," Silas interjected, tilting his head, "but I shall not breathe a word on pain of death! And..." a sly smile played on his lips "and with Morbid around that is always in one's mind."

James didn't seem to hear, his hand covering Marianne's own.

Outside a door slammed, echoing painfully and fragmenting any thoughts he was about to voice. Silas and Marianne turned in tandem.

Then there was white. So much white.

James heard a voice, muffled through a blanket he had over his head, casually dropped by a heedless hand. He found the darkness and the claustrophobic confines oddly comforting. Slowly he hooked the corner and pulled it off, his skin pale as always, used to heat and tolerant of cold it seldom changed in colour to match the atmosphere.

The grizzled face of the doctor was the last thing he wished to see when the blanket was pulled down and the realisation that he was still on the cold floor outside his room was equally unnerving.

"I-I'm fine," James struggled into a sitting position, rubbing his tired temples. "I felt dizzy, perhaps I have not been eating correctly or nor sleeping enough."

"Is that so?" Morbridge smirked cynically as he watched the awkward manoeuvre. "For a glorious moment I thought I may have a new study."

"No one is here for your study!" James snapped as he gripped the door handle, easing himself up. "Or even because they want to be, who would want to be sat in filth? We live, we breathe, even if that ends too soon for certain people."

The implication was clear but the words had no effect, only widening the smile on the others face.

"What else is there to do with them?" Morbridge asked frankly as he got to his feet, brushing away the clinging dust on his trousers, his dark eyes watching the man's every movement. "Their minds are as barren as a wombless woman, occasionally a phantom seed is sown but a phantom is all it is. When the mind fails, humanity ends."

James shook his head as he pushed open his door, not allowing the sharp words he wished to say to leave his lips.

No words could break the iron will of the doctor, his mind set, and attempting to change it would be as futile as trying to turn the tide.

It meant he would have to discover his humanity and that was something he would never do.

"If you say so," he said dismissively, "but if I am to speak honestly even animals receive basic care better than this."

A smirk twisted the others thin lips. "Animals serve a purpose."

James held the obdurate gaze with a pitying one of his own. Pity worked far better than hatred in such circumstances.

"Does turning a blind eye to the suffering around you erase the inhumanity? Or does it merely make you just like the monsters you seek to avoid?"

The exchange of eyes lasted for some seconds before the doctor sniffed and turned on his heel without another word, striding down the stairway with his footsteps echoing behind him.

Waiting until the sound faded before he stepped back into his room James looked over his shoulder at the familiar surroundings. After all this agitation the dull and uncomfortable room felt like the finest suite in the grandest hotel.

Or it would have been if he could abolish the cold and the sounds of human suffering from the atmosphere. The latter he believed were now embedded in his mind, never to be erased.

A glimmer of light managed to squeeze through the barriers outside and a flicker caught his eye from under the bed.

He frowned.

Moving over he knelt down, ignoring the cramp in his legs from the coldness of the floor, to pull out the cause of the shimmer.

His hands shook as they touched the strange smoothness and pulled out the container.

Turning it over he looked at the syrupy liquid that undulated in the base. Sweat appeared on his brow, despite the chill in the air, as he recognised it. The medicine from what he believed to have been an illusion.

He took a short breath and stood abruptly, opening his drawer with similar force to drop the offending container into the dark, slamming it shut.

"Utter lunacy!" he muttered irritably, sitting heavily on the protesting mattress and looking up into the shadows that clung to the wall. "I don't believe in spirits or ghouls! This is ridiculous!"

His voice was stronger and the tone bitter but inside his heart that too was a farce. He wished he could, like the scientists who tore through the veils of knowledge, convince himself that if something were not explainable then it simply did not exist.

If there was a logical explanation to all this then it was beyond his sight.

Chapter Seventeen

'He does not know.'

Silas looked up from prone position on his bed. After all this time he never had gotten used to hearing a disembodied voice.

And answering to it without speaking aloud was equally difficult but the thought of what the other warders would think should they hear him talking to himself made on try harder.

'Not yet. Let us be honest, Marianne, would *you*? Our minds may be deemed irreparable but common sense still prevails to most.'

There was silence for some time and he thought she had terminated the conversation. She rarely sent a farewell, she simply ended it.

But as he settled back, toying with the blunt pencil held in slender fingers, her voice filled his head once more.

'Will he ever?'

Silas pondered the question, three simple words that stumped him.

"I don't know. Hope springs eternal?" He twirled the pencil in his hair. "God's will and all that."

'God's will,' Marianne repeated thoughtfully with a soft hum *'and also his own.'*

"Aye."

A soft, indistinct murmur was the only response before silence once again fell and it was clear that time that the woman was not going to speak again.

• • •

Morbridge knew Nathaniel would be on alert even before the door was opened. With his sight taken his hearing had become far sharper. So much so he knew who was coming by the pattern of the gait alone.

Rather irksome for the doctor who did enjoy the panic of surprise but it was also intriguing how the human body adapted to its situations.

He had barely opened the door a fraction before he heard the rich tones of the inmate's voice, soft and almost sultry.

"Hello, doctor."

Morbridge gave a grunt in acknowledgment, standing silently with his weighty gaze penetrating into the tethered man.

Nathaniel could feel the heaviness of the poisonous eyes but gave no sign of nervousness.

"To what do I owe this visit?" he finally asked, tilting his head in the doctor's direction. "I cannot recall you ever gracing my presence unless you really have to. It is almost like you are *afraid*."

An angry scowl furrowed the doctor's brow but he kept his temper. With Nathaniel it was safer not to, he knew the man's temperament far more than the warders. Instead he folded his arms and leant against the opposite wall, his eyes never leaving the patient.

"You know why, Nathaniel."

"Do I indeed? We've spoken seldom, Doctor and although our few conversations have been long they have also been inane and imbecilic medical blather and theories that your own mind concocts to further your ambition." He smirked. "Ashes in the water and ashes in the sea but none jump back up for none can flee."

"Yes, well. You cannot expect any progress without loss and animals have differing systems. One finds out far more from a human specimen."

A low laugh echoed eerily, a laugh that made even Morbridge's skin prickle as if shards of ice pierced it.

"You go back to the counting house to count out the money, money taken from corpses, isn't that funny?"

Morbridge made a face, eyebrows knitting together in disapproval but he wouldn't allow it to provoke him.

He gave an airy shrug.

"They cannot take worldly goods to the grave and none come forth the claim them or the mortal remains so what else is to be done? Give it to a poor house for their staff to squander on gin and gambling? I think not."

Nathaniel made a sound that seemed to be a combination of a growl and a chuckle, rocking back against his bounds, rattling like a ghoul in chains.

"Money and gold corrupts man more than Satan himself, each coin gained means ten more are desired."

"There are far more important things I want, Nathaniel," Morbridge snapped irritably, bending down to seize the already taut ropes, tugging them harshly. Blood flowed from already chafed wrists but the man simply laughed once again as he felt the warm trickle down his skin.

"Blood makes such pretty art," he whispered, tracing his finger on the floor in congruent with the small river. "Such art can be created but never bought. But tell me the reason for your visit, before your actions provoke my creative side."

He felt the doctor's breath caress his cheek as he leant forward, the scent pungent as though the man had absorbed the chemical's he worked so close to.

"I need your talents, my dear Atrocity."

Nathaniel snorted, pulling his head away in an arrogant toss.

"Indeed. Well, my *talents*, as you term them, are fickle. Quite contrary if you life, only my pretty maids were not buried in a garden."

"Not just maids, so the theory goes," Morbridge answered deliberately, "it seems your only stipulations for your victims was blonde hair."

"No, there was more to it than that but I don't expect someone with no creativity to understand my reasons," Nathaniel sounded indignant, almost insulted at the assumption. "Outer looks are petty and blondes are *very* petty. But a man of words and not of deeds is like a garden full of weeds," he gave a cruel smirk "and weeds should not be allowed to grow."

"You make no sense," Morbridge moved back with a contemptuous sniff, "but you rarely do, like the other incompetents here, but you have skills that they do not. If I am to obtain the control and note that I want then I reluctantly accept I must take help."

Nathaniel rocked back, the rattle of restraints a welcome distraction from what would have been a suffocating silence.

After a moment he stopped abruptly and Morbridge felt the weight of a hidden gaze, contemplating his words. Eventually a soft and intrigued response left his lips.

"What's in it for me?"

Chapter Eighteen

The corridor was eerily silent as James made his way down towards the partition between the ward for the sexes.

He knew it was forbidden but he needed to see Marianne again, her presence comforting, her calmness, despite her situation, reassuring.

The lack of sound unnerved him and his eyes fixed themselves on the cold, stone floor, fearful of looking into the rooms.

His hand played with the strange container concealed in his jacket pocket, not willing to risk leaving it in view or even hidden lest someone find it.

It felt like months since he had found it and perhaps it had been. Time made no sense here, days and hours seemed nonexistent, day and night rolled into one.

No wonder his memory seemed to fail him.

He pulled out the medication and looked at it, watching the sap like liquid slowly sway in the container.

It sickened him.

'I can throw it away when I next go to the well for the water,' he thought, shoving it back and out of sight. 'Toss it over the wall and leave it to the woods to deal with. I can but hope that it does not reappear afterwards.'

The sooner the better, the container was an obvious bulge in his pocket and he didn't want the hassle of awkward questions.

His pace quickened, his head dropping down to blind himself to the dark and silence, keeping his mind on his destination.

It was risky. Men were, for both dignity and decency, forbidden to enter the female quarters unless otherwise instructed.

That moral code was often ignored and James ha the inkling that unwanted pregnancies happened all too often, at least he was certain he'd heard that from somewhere.

Yet one more thing he wasn't sure of. This place, it drained the memory as well as any remnants of sanity people had.

Their ailments were not catching but they weighed heavy on one's person and in the very air around them, the burden threatening to take him down as well.

His focus returned to Marianne, how her silent company eased the tension, how her strange conversation methods soothed the highest-strung nerves.

He'd known someone like that in the past. A thought that made him wince, the realisation of how much he couldn't recall was bothersome.

He paused in the vestibule. An empty room with only a ragged rug to fill the void and a door that led into the thick of the forest, not that it was often used, so seldom was it opened the hinges were rusted.

The back doors, facing the mainland, barely visible due to the veil of mist and sea spray, were the ones normally opened to admit new unfortunates and take delivery of supplies. Not that he could recall ever seeing anyone or anything, his mind as blank as the dark ocean surrounding them.

For a minute he rested his eyes, feeling them burn behind the lids before exhaling slowly.

'...so confident as a child. Why doesn't he use it now?'

The mismatched eyes snapped open; the voice so clear as though the speaker was directly next to him.

He felt a brief breeze as if someone had walked past him or away from him but there was nothing.

Shaking his head, he moved on, his pace quicker than before and a cold chill nesting in his body.

• • •

Marianne was sat quietly, her slim legs pulled to her chest and her hands pulling the skirt of the thin garment down to cover herself as best she could.

The dress gave little dignity but she would keep what was left of her pride, not forget it as so many unfortunates had done before her.

A tiny smile graced her lip as she heard the overly cautious footsteps. It became so easy to identify a person by that sound alone.

At the sound of the lock being opened as quietly as the man could manage she shifted, lowering her legs to curl them beneath her, a position more suited to a welcome guest, her eyes bright and almost eager as she watched the door.

It opened just enough to allow the man to enter, slipping through shakily but her calmness seemed to ease his nerves.

"I shouldn't be here I know," James said, biting his bottom lip, "but in some ways it feels safer to come here, there seems to be less staff."

In fact, he couldn't remember seeing any except when he was sent to deliver the records to the formidable matron.

Marianne patted the bed beside her, her eyes filled with warmth and an inner glow of happiness that could rival the joy of sunny day.

James sat on the end of the bed, not wishing to encroach on her personal space. The fabric was damp and cold, saturated by the moisture that crept through the cold walls. Up close and coherent he could see the thin garment she wore was not much better, clinging to her flesh, the swell of her breast and almost transparent in parts.

Swallowing his embarrassment he looked down at the floor, focusing as if the scraps of straw and dust were as fascinating as a Monet.

'You need not blush.'

Marianne's amused tone caused his eyes to shift up, meeting her smiling orbs twinkling in the gloom.

'A body is flesh and flesh is human, I am just scars and skin, covered enough to be decent.'

She reached out to rest a cool hand on his own, his fingers taut as they gripped nothing, a slight flicker of a flinch twitching the skin as he felt the touch.

'You are wise but you have so much to learn.'

"I did need to be told that," James answered weakly "I already know. One thing I actually am aware of."

He ran his free hand roughly through his hair as if about to tear the blonde locks from his head, exposing both eyes to the world for a brief moment.

"I feel like I am losing my mind, seeing things like mirages in a desert, it all seems too real though. The changes in the building, rooms shifting," his breath quickened as he spoke, his throat feeling constricted as the words tumbled from him "one day feels like another and time makes no sense…"

He bit down on his lip, stopping the ramble in mid flow. He was beginning to sound unhinged even to himself let alone any who could have overheard.

Marianne pressed a finger to her cheek, her thoughts silent. Her gaze had slipped into the distance but a shimmer in her eyes betrayed a wise woman trapped in her mute form. Her fingers traced his own in calming, circular motions and instead of words she hummed a sweet sound in her mind, one James seemed to know but had lost somewhere in the past.

Giving a long breath James continued, mustering all his self-control and banishing the irksome nerves that plagued him. This wasn't like him. He knew that somehow.

"Still," he managed a smile "I am not here to bother you with my tale of woe, it'll pass soon enough. I'm just tired I suppose; you know I don't get that much help from the other warders."

'It is not weakness to admit you have flaws, that you fear and struggle,' Marianne's voice echoed through him with a reverential care, 'it is human.'

"Human. Yes," James nodded listlessly, "and humans tear so easily."

Marianne looked at him with sympathy but said nothing else, resting her head gently against his shoulder.

A soft hum filled his mind again as she sent out another tune, slow and soothing. She made up her own songs and music to pass the dragging time but they were songs never to be heard in the outside world.

James was one of her chosen few who were given the opportunity to listen to her melodies. Songs that had gotten her through the rough and the painful, hoping they would have the same pacifying effect on him as they had on her.

The thoughts still ruminated around James's head like moths about a flame but the soulful music touched his heart. Whilst some invited the body to dance this implored it to relax and it did so without any effort.

James did not want to ask her where her skill came from but Marianne already guessed.

'I used to tend to my siblings when they could not sleep,' she explained so quietly the words barely registered in his mind. 'Two of them were sickly, as if they had not been born whole in body or mind. Someone needed to ease their fears as they approached Heaven and mother wasn't able, she would not accept them. I helped with all my siblings.'

"I used to know a girl like that in my schooldays," James replied thoughtlessly, "at least I'm certain I did, I just feel it."

A budding seed of a memory that refused to blossom but always there, pushing at the surface.

'Yes.'

He looked at Marianne who gave a strange and ambiguous smile. It sent a chill through his body, not pleasant but not *un*pleasant either.

It was just peculiar, a tingling sensation from his gut and up his spine.

"Yes," he repeated, drawing the word out to a hiss. His arm slipped about her waist but his eyes remained fixed in the shadows, "whatever that means now."

And then came the white. So much white.

Muffled, disembodied voices and strange sounds echoing around him as though he were in a tunnel. An all too bright tunnel. He felt arms entwine about him, thin and almost skeletal, Marianne's sweet perfume fading to something sharper and more potent like the chemicals meant to cleanse the filth from the floors.

And silence.

. . .

The sun rose high, red and vibrant as it stained a rocky ocean and trickled through the dense trees that surrounded the island like impenetrable walls.

A thin rivulet squeezed through the bars that caged the inmates and separated them from any clear view of daylight or the world outside.

James's eyes felt as though leaden weights had been inserted beneath the lids and stung as though he hadn't blinked all night. The burn of the light made them even worse, worse than the whiteness that had penetrated his mind all night.

Marianne still leant against him, her own eyes shut but whether she slept or simply drifted was debatable. Her breathing had calmed to the tranquillity of slumber but her body was less so, ready to jolt into wakefulness at any sound.

"I have to get back," James muttered tiredly as he gently removed his tense arm from about her, his muscles aching from holding his position so long.

Marianne's eyes opened and she nodded once, the smile still on her lips, the knowing expression still present.

"I just hope no one noticed my absence, I will have to forge my checks but nothing ever seems to occur on my rounds, if the fates are in my favour then that luck will hold."

He clasped her hand as he stood, holding the delicate fingers as though they were made of porcelain, meeting her gaze and feeling his pulse in his throat.

"I will get back to you, I just wish I could set you free from here," he whispered mournfully "you do not belong in this makeshift prison."

'The only prison is fear and to free yourself and perhaps others you must overcome that darkness and doubt.'

James reached to stroke the wan cheek, leaning over gracelessly to press a chaste kiss to the cool forehead, his hand caressing her thinning hair.

"Thank you," he spoke so softly it was a wonder her breath did not drown his words "I can but try but fear is a powerful enemy. But if tales have told us anything it is that most foes can be defeated."

A slim arm embraced him with skeletal grace as she rocked against him, clinging to the safety and warmth he emanated, feeling the beat of his pulse, reminding her that life was not all despair and pain.

James's arms moved about her shoulders, holding her rather awkwardly. He could not recall being close to a female before, not in a way that made his heart palpitate in such a manner. In the back of his mind he seemed to sense a sororal fondness but no more.

"I have to go," he repeated although he made no move to release her. It was Marianne who reluctantly pulled away, pressing his hand to her lips in a farewell gesture.

Swallowing the mass of emotions that formed a lump in his throat James stepped away, keeping his eyes upon her until he reached the door and had to turn away.

Chapter Nineteen

James reached his room without encountering anyone. The entire building seemed silent, even the wind outside gave no sound as it swept through the trees.

A sense of foreboding engulfed his senses as he approached the door, the once welcome sight now causing him to want to turn and flee.

That was not his nature though, to run from trouble. And even if it was, he could not do that forever, facing things was far more beneficial.

He gave a sigh of exasperation and wrenched the door open, waiting in the coldness of the corridor would do no good and he simply ran the risk of becoming ill. Working was taxing enough without the feeling of one's lungs being wrenched from the body or their head throbbing.

At first glance nothing seemed out of place. The bedclothes were creased on the bed with his spare clothes just as he'd left it and the drawers had not been touched.

A chill breeze wisped through the window and brought goose bumps to his skin. Or perhaps that was just his anxiety manifesting more clearly.

Shaking his head at his foolishness he wandered inside, closing the door to keep the access cold out, leaning against the frame as he continued his scrutiny of the familiar room that seemed so alien at that moment. His suspicions that something was amiss were still high even though his eyes failed to spot anything.

Feeling for the jar he forced his gaze away as he pulled it from his pocket. He wrinkled his nose and tossed it over onto the mattress, immediately following when a rustle sounded instead of a soft thud.

With a frown he moved over, whipping the blanket from the bed and sending the container flying into the corner with a clatter. Amazingly it didn't shatter.

On the bed was a folded piece of paper, the former rips and creases still clear on its surface.

James felt a combined sense of anger, irritation and anxiety as he approached robotically, his feet moving forward on their own accord. He already knew what it would be before he even opened it, in many ways that was a blessing and limited the shock.

He opened it with a single flick of his wrist, faced once again with the childish drawing. And once again it was altered.

The adult figures had almost faded from view; the faintest of outlines remained as though someone attempted to erase them and left only the indent from the pencil. The children's faces had fallen, looking almost sad or afraid, their eyes bigger.

He gazed at it for some minutes, shaking his head slowly. How many more times did he need to attempt to dispose of it? It was beginning to feel as though it was cursed and unable to be destroyed.

Opening his hand he let it float to the floor, pushing it under the bed to collect dust and hopefully be forgotten. If he couldn't rid himself of it then the best he could do was eradicate it from his sight and hopefully his memory.

Leaning down he picked up the discarded blanket and shook it open, humming the same tune Marianne had gifted to him as he folded it back onto the bed, smoothing the creases carefully even if they would reappear as soon as he sat down.

He didn't remember lying down or falling asleep. Yet when the banging on the door jolted him back to reality he was on the bed and looking at the ceiling.

The bang came again, sounding more impatient as the person banged their fist against the rickety frame.

'Can you get that? I'm busy.'

"Alright, alright!" James grumbled as he rolled over, his eyes feeling as if burning embers smouldered behind them. "Give me a minute!"

He frowned as he sat up before dismissing the feminine voice, simply the residue of an already forgotten dream.

Reaching for the handle the door was practically pulled open for him, revealing the impatient figure of his fellow worker, tapping his foot testily.

"Doctor wants to see you," he said in a surly tone, turning to leave as soon as the words left him, "so move it, he's in a bad mood as always."

James shook his head, apparently it was going to be one of those days when he was forced to proceed with a permanent headache and one that was likely to be worse by the time his shift was due.

• • •

Morbridge's office was small but sumptuously decorated.

A bookcase full of expensive tomes lined the left side, weighted with knowledge and facts, their gilt gold titles catching the light of fireplace opposite, a beautiful oil painting hanging above it.

All his furniture was dark, polished mahogany or other wealthy woods, his seats lined with deep violet velvet. All luxuries that befitted his status or what he believed was his status.

Despite the opulence it was devoid of any personal effects that would give any insight to the man behind the career. It was purely a space of business and a showroom of grossly gained prestige. And despite his bluster and bravado he would never dare show what trinkets he did possess, taken from the dead and dying and even those who still lived. To him they were as good as corpses anyway.

James perched uncomfortably on the harder seat by the desk, knitting his fingers together nervously while Morbridge continued with documenting his latest doings in no particular hurry.

It felt like an age before the man finally laid down the pen and lifted his dark eyes slowly, the gas light above making them glow in a sinister fashion.

For a few seconds the doctor gazed at him studiously, each tick of the clock feeling like an hour. James shifted, looking the very image of a wayward schoolboy in the masters' presence.

"Are you like Judas, Grey?" he asked in a low, baleful voice. "Feigning loyalty when you heart holds fast to betrayal?"

"I don't know, or care to know, what that means," James replied readily, "but I never took you for a religious man, Sir."

Morbridge wrinkled his nose, the contempt shining brightly from his demeanour. The sudden nerve had taken him aback and that alone lowered the other in his eyes.

"I'm not. However, I work with those who are and you pick up names and phrases the longer you allow those delusions to rot their brains. Imbecilic as I find such things it is all they have to hold to."

"That aside," James sat back, attempting to portray a calm and composed figure even though the feeling of unease was viscera,l "what exactly did you want to see me about that was so urgent?"

With a sigh Morbridge leaned on his desk, pressing his hands together, his eyes never leaving the man before him, taking in every movement and blink of his eyes.

"I will keep things short since you don't seem entirely awake," he said curtly. "Last night a few things went missing, small in quantity they all add up and I am not about to postulate a theory on the supernatural." He fixed his stony gaze upon the smaller male as if trying to crush him with the weight of that alone. "Where were you last night?"

"Doing my normal mundane duties," James responded stiltedly, immediately thinking of the vial in his possession. "I don't know where else you'd expect me to be. And if you want to know if I saw or recall anything then no, I don't."

He couldn't reveal where he had been, a secret it had to stay.

Morbridge sat back again with a stiff smile, one that made even the strongest baulk.

"You don't recall much, do you? I have heard rumours of your forgetfulness for a while now."

"We all have those days, Sir, I don't see anything unusual or concerning about it."

111

"In the case of a normal person then it would be a trifling matter," Morbridge said as he tapped a blunt nail on the arm of the chair "but you, *you* have shown to be less than normal."

James's eyes darkened as he met the man's stare, his lips tightening. He didn't respond, not willing to rise to the bait like a fish to a worm.

"You know I am partial to the abnormalities in the human species," Morbridge continued. "I can't help but wonder of your eyes are key to the flaws in your mind that you're beginning to show. Had you been an inmate you would have been a prime specimen for research, in fact you still could be."

Automatically James adjusted the lopsided fringe, an act that only increased the unpleasant smirk the doctor sported.

"My eyes are my own and have nothing to do with you!" he stated forcibly. "I may not be fond of them but I do value the sight they give."

At least when they served their true purpose of seeing what was actually real.

"Yes, well if you ever change your mind I trust you'll let me know?"

"I assure you that will be unlikely, Sir."

Morbridge smiled coldly, lowering his voice to a direful hiss.

"You might not have to grant permission," his eyes shone with ghoulish intent. "Continue on this path, my friend, and you may find your status here alters dramatically."

James gave a sniff of disregard but inside his breast his heart palpitated fearfully. He had hoped any difference in his behaviour or mood had not been apparent, he rarely conferred with the others and nor they with him.

"Word has reached my keen ears that delusions have begun to affect you, a sad risk of working amongst those who suffer them."

James gave no response, only a slight shrug of his shoulders. The young warder did not want to add more smoke to the fire, albeit a dead one, any words would most likely be twisted to give credence to the rumours.

112

"You have nothing to add? Well, nothing comes from nothing, Grey," Morbridge crowed, a smug smile tilting his lips, "but I cannot force your words as yet."

He held his gaze for some moments before giving an abrupt gesture of his hand.

"And nothing comes from idle speculation either, Sir," James retorted, standing abruptly, the chair rocking precariously as he did. "I bid you good day but beware Doctor, even the strongest of minds are not a fortress."

"Perhaps not. But some are far better armed than others," Morbridge responded placidly, flicking his hand as though swatting a fly. "Now go, however we shall certainly meet again."

James left, not staying to even comment. Regardless of his tiredness that would almost certainly hinder his duties later he headed outside to the courtyard.

He stood in the coolness of the doorway and listened to the mighty roar of the tides beyond, sounding as though Leviathan himself stirred below and made the island tremble.

The air was clammy as it mingled with the spray and droplets blowing from the leaning trees, clinging to his skin.

He scraped his heel on the ground, tracing a pattern on the cobbles, worn from the rain and sleet and the tread of the many feet that had walked them.

The wind died down for a brief moment, giving an almost blissful silence until another sound, far more alien, penetrated it.

A soft and sorrowful sob drifting from the direction of the lonely well, a sound that chilled his heart and core.

Regardless of his nerves James's curiosity pushed him forward, his feet seeming to gain weight with every step until he reached the low brim, his fingers curling around the damp lips as he peered into the dark maws.

Nothing. Not a ripple.

He blinked. Bemused but relieved having not been certain how he would have reacted to seeing a face staring back from the blackness below.

'Come home again. I know you can hear!'

A bead of sweat trickled from his brow, circling down his cheek. He took a deep breath.

"Ridiculous!" he muttered crossly to himself, his pace quickening as he headed back towards the drier, although not warmer, building. "You're letting your imagination run away again, damned doctors."

'James...'

He ignored it. It was not Marianne and it whilst it sounded oddly familiar it was purely a tired fancy and sleep, if it would come to him, would drive such things away.

'Ja...'

The voice died as the door swung shut.

Chapter Twenty

As soon as James saw his door was ajar he knew something was wrong. No one entered his room except him, giving it a wide berth. None ever came this way unless they had to, there was no need.

Pushing the door he detected a subtle, acrid scent, similar to the phenol he often smelt seeping from the medical rooms to try and disguise the sickly odour of blood.

Peering around the door everything looked tidy. His bed smoothed over and a blanket folded on the end that he had never laid eyes on before. To him that made it even more curious, why should anyone want to pass by and adjust things?

Moving across he flicked it back but nothing lay under the alien fabric, just the bedding with the few creases that were unable to be smoothed out by whoever's hand had touched it. James ran his fingers over the cover lightly as if searching for unseen clues but finding none.

Giving a sigh he shook his head, leaning on the mattress with his fists.

"Maybe this is simple paranoia," he mused aloud, looking about the room. "I…"

He paused when he caught sight of the bedside cabinet, the middle drawer open a mere crack when it had been shut fast when he had left.

Reaching over he wrenched it open, the hinges resisting the abrupt pull. He quite expected to see the drawing laying there and part of him was intrigued to see how it had altered, if it had.

There it lay, cradled by emptiness, but that was not what drew his eyes. What pulled his gaze was the dust-free outline of where his knife was once sat.

He felt himself pale, felt the blood drain from his veins and the cold settle as he reached out to press his fingertips to the cool wood to check that he was not just imagining its absence. He almost wished he was but the feel of the rough wood indicated otherwise.

"How..." He trailed away, why bother asking a meaningless question that could not be answered?

He ran his hand through his hair, gripping the blond locks as if he was about to pull them out by the roots, the subtle pain indicating he was still awake and, odd and it was, enabled him to think more clearly.

"It can't be far," he muttered breathily, needing to break the cold silence even if it was just with the sound of his own voice. "Simply misplaced. Yes, that must be it! I moved it. Knowing my luck I'll find it when I tread or sit on the damn thing."

There weren't many places in here it could be, retracing his steps outside of the room was of no use, he'd never taken the item from here. The results of wandering with a blade would be devastating if one of the more violent patients seized it.

A thorough search was to no avail. He checked every crack and crevice, even moving the bed to sift the gathered dust that settled immediately after displacement.

Not was the bedding itself spared, stripped and searched before being redressed in a haphazard manner.

With a grunt of frustration he sat down heavily, the legs of the bed screeching as it was forced back to its original place.

The soft pad of footfalls piqued his attention and he looked over to the door, soft voices mingled with them, intermittent and dissonant like the crackling of a fire it was hard to make out what they said.

The gentler lilt indicated a female but that was all he was able to discern with the door muffling the noises.

Giving a sigh James pulled himself to his feet and opened the door. Immediately the noises ceased and nothing was out of place.

Just dust dancing in the sparse light.

He bit his lip in irritation at his active imagination. Phantasm it might be, it was still irksome and made him feel as though his own mind slipped away.

As he turned back to try and get some sleep he noticed a movement from the corner of his eyes, a soft white hue moving in stark contrast to the black of the shadows.

James squinted and inched forward in an attempt to see the blurred figure better, at least he assumed it was a figure, could just be yet another fanciful illusion but the more he looked he knew this could be no case of simple pareidolia.

As his sight adjusted he could make out the form of the woman. The white of the dress was dulled by a cream hued jacket that tapered off just above her thigh. Her eyes looked up, glittering as though they were wet with unspent tears, but while she looked at him it felt she didn't see him. Not the real person who stood before her.

'I hope you hear, I try so hard,' the lips moved but the words were not in tandem and reminded him of a bad ventriloquist. *'All I can do is try, try and hope. I keep telling myself "one day", and one day has to come eventually.'*

She shrugged her slim shoulders, the dress rippling around her legs like a thick mist, fading in and out from his vision.

Her words seemed to jumble as her form flickered statically, a holographic trick that was failing in power.

'One day, someday,' she continued, her voice becoming a quieter sigh as she began to fade from view, the white the last thing to vanish. *'One day.'*

James's gaze remained fixed on where she had been, chills cooling the blood in his veins as he tried to make sense of the words, to connect them with reality. However hard he tried it seemed impossible and with a toss of his head he strode back into his room, shutting the door firmly behind him.

Sleep would not come easily, the strange chemical smell still hanging in the air and the room feeling more uncomfortable with the knowledge that someone else may have been in there, touching his things and smoothing the bed where he lay.

When sleep finally came it was heavy and would give little sense of rest when he awoke.

A rustle of paper stirred him, followed by a loud, single bang on the door. A groan left him as he rolled over, knocking the flattened pillow to the floor as he struggled to sit up. Before he could respond a voice boomed just as loudly.

"Will you move your damned backside? You've got extra work since one of the others has gone off sick! No doubt caught some damn disease from these retarded creatures."

"At least they have decency," James muttered under his breath. "Most are more human than those who work here."

Clearing his throat he lifted his voice to call out although he barely seemed loud enough to be heard over the soft rustle of his nightshirt pooling at his feet.

"He's probably gotten a chill; I don't know about your rooms but if they are as cold as this one I'm surprised it isn't pneumonia."

Whoever was outside paced impatiently, cursing under his breath before his footsteps began to walk away.

"Left your list on the door, just hurry up, otherwise you'll have the doctor on your case!"

James bit back a caustic retort and dressed himself with aching muscles, the product of an uncomfortable and heavy sleep.

He tore the paper from where it had been impaled on the handle, barely glancing at it. His own list alone was enough and took much of the evening to complete. Depending on the circumstances of the patients even an extra three or four could take up a lot of time.

Instinctively his step slowed as he approached where the figure from the night before had stood, the air feeling oddly colder there than anywhere else. He reached out as if extending his arm to clasp an invisible hand but met nothing, not that he expected to.

Moving through the cold patch he looked down at the list, cringing when he saw not only had he five extra checks to perform but Nathaniel's name was listed in bolder pen.

"I should have known," he muttered sullenly. "Who else would have done it?"

No one that was who and despite his loathing of the man someone had to check he hadn't injured himself in some manner.

The awful thought that they wouldn't be that fortunate floated through his mind, Nathaniel wouldn't be as gracious to give them that reprieve.

It was hard to stifle the feeling of growing anxiety as he made his way down the stairway, whiteness flashing in his peripheral vision as the light reflected from the metal. That seldom happened and outside was dark; it made little sense as the moon was never that bright due to the closeness of the trees.

His hand tightened on the railing, attempting to ignore the flashes that seemed to contain images, faces that were left etched in his eyes when he blinked. Blank faces with distorted features, only their being clear, gaping black holes in an otherwise flat portrait.

Pausing on the last step he rubbed his eyes, trying to rid them of both the images and the headache they were beginning to cause.

As his vision cleared his looked back at the list, Nathaniel's name more prominent than the rest which appeared smeared and unreadable beside his.

The words seemed to shift and dance on the paper, the black of the ink seeping away to leave red stains in its wake, coppery hues that resembled dried blood. It looked so real that James could almost feel the paper become saturated with sticky fluid before drying; he threw it from him in disgust.

It floated lethargically down to the floor and landed pristine, not a sign of gore or even a smudge of ink.

James left it there, marking it with a shoeprint as his foot crushed it, grinding the edge with the dull heel as he strode away.

Chapter Twenty-One

James met no one on his walk to the basement areas where the worst of their afflicted were stowed away from sight even if not from mind.

The air was still and the as quiet as a tomb as he made his way down the dark stairwell. He gripped the cold banister, unaccustomed to the steps.

All the cells were empty; their doors wide like the maws of a beast awaiting naïve prey. All James could hope that he wasn't blindly walking into hidden claws. He heard the faint clink of iron chains as he neared the room, any gentle shift would rattle them, alerting whoever passed to his movement. Or lack of it.

The latter being preferable to the former.

Flicking back the hatch James peered through, waiting a moment for his eyes to adjust to the gloom of the room within.

Nathaniel sat motionless, his head hanging down as though asleep, suspended only by the tethers that bound him. With the blindfold over his eyes it was impossible to tell.

The man seemed to be fond of feigning slumber when he was awake and highly alert. Only the rise and fall of his chest gave any indication to his state.

James unlocked the door with shaking hands, fingers finding it hard to grip the keys they held. As the door creaked open Nathaniel's head jerked up, clattering the chains that held him. James jolted, his heart pounding against his ribcage.

He took a bolstering breath, a bead of nervous sweat trickling down his brow and dropping onto the floor. Nathaniel's shifted, looking towards where the droplet had fallen, a soft chuckle vibrating from his throat.

"Oh I so adore the glorious scent of fear penetrating the air," he said with a low aroused groan, "almost as much as the scent of blood and death," he rocked slowly, gyrating the chains. "When your fear begins to smart it's like penknife to your heart and when that heart begins to bleed you're dead, you're dead, you're dead indeed!"

James stared at him in silence, his lungs feeling as though they lacked the ability to draw breath let alone the air to reply.

He could feel Nathaniel watching in his blinded way, smelling the nerves that permeated from every pore in his body.

"No knife, literal or metaphorical, has pierced me yet," he said curtly as he moved across to check the cleanliness of the room. "And nor will it."

"Will it not? Your family left you; your friends let you bleed so sleep tight with a knife for that's all you need?" Nathaniel shifted himself and a flash of silver reflected from the chains as a knife dropped from his person. "Missing something? Among other things."

James felt his heart still and his blood cool in his veins as he looked at the familiar blade that lay on the stone.

"How did you...?" He stuttered, closing his eyes for a brief moment to bring himself under some control. "You cannot move!"

"Do not underestimate what I can or cannot do," Nathaniel sneered maliciously "all you see could just be a strange illusion."

James edged forward; moving to take back the blade lest anyone else find it and more suspicion was put upon his shoulders. There was no such thing of innocent until proven guilty, it was quite the opposite and should this be found there would be no way to prove his innocence.

As he bent down Nathaniel gave a roll of his lower body, pushing the blade beneath him and out of reach.

"Try it," Nathaniel hissed between clenched teeth. "They don't believe anything you say, you're already proving yourself as one of us! You're in the records, warden!"

"I am nothing like you!"

Anger radiated off James in waves and his hand connected

with Nathaniel's cheek with a resounding crack, a scarlet imprint staining the white skin.

Instead of seeming shocked, sounding pained, the man laughed, a low rumbling sound like the thunder that rocked the island.

"You think you are safe? You should not judge by what you first see."

"Little else I can do with you Nathaniel," James ejected bitterly, nursing his hand, the knuckles painful from the blow.

"Perhaps not."

The despisal in James's eyes was hard enough to be seen even through the blindfold and judging from the malevolent grin it seemed it was.

The air in the room seemed to grow heavy as he stood there, his feet seeming to have lost the ability to move. When he forced them on it was as though he was walking through quicksand, the thought he could sink deeper spurring him leave.

Nathaniel had become still, frozen in place but as James moved past his hand flew out, clamping down on his wrist with an iron grip, his fingers cold and unbreakable.

"Sight can be deceiving."

James's heart palpitated in a blend of anticipation and dread as all he could do was watch as Nathaniel stood, the chains falling limply to the floor in a violent crash of steel. His free hand tore the tattered blindfold from flint grey eyes that blinked in disconcertion as the slight increase of light.

When James's eyes locked with his, the reason for his condition was clear, his gaze so intense it froze his soul.

There was no humanity in them.

A low rumbling chuckle bubbled out from Nathaniel's throat, the sound of a rabid animal. James felt icy tendrils wrap themselves about his heart, his throat constricted, making it hard even to gulp back the bile that rose upwards, the sound of the inner mechanisms working in his throat distinct in the silence.

"You…"

"Shut your mouth or I'll cut it from ear to ear!" Nathaniel

snarled, shifting his head to where the knife lay in the corner, eyes as bright as the blade itself. "And who will they blame?"

James's eyes burned with anger and suppressed tears of both rage and panic as the hand closed over his throat, pressing hard against his jugular and cutting off any words that tried to pass his lips.

He felt his pulse throb harder under the calloused fingertips, frantic and desperate like the fluttering of an ensnared bird.

The air seemed frigid as several moments passed by but Nathaniel's steely gaze suddenly dropped and his grip slackened.

"No. I don't kill children."

He sank back down. Had it not been for the restraints piled on the floor it appeared as though he had never moved at all.

"I am *not* a child," James whispered after sucking in as much air as he could into his deprived lungs.

Nathaniel looked vacantly at him but made no response.

Inching forward James leant down to retrieve the knife, his hand glossy with sweat and shaking as he picked it up and slipped it into his pocket, the hilt protruding from the top.

He expected the overt show of dread to provoke amusement in the savage beast that sat unchained but if he had noticed he made no sign as if he was frozen in place.

James watched him for a moment like a doe in the sights of a predator, an attack inevitable but powerless to move.

When nothing happened, the man remained as still as stone, he slowly back away towards the door, the silence ominous.

He waved his hand fleetingly before the unblinking eyes, the gaze as still as the rest of him.

His feet echoed softly as he backed from the door, letting it swing shut with an almighty crash.

And then there was white.

Chapter Twenty-Two

James found himself back in his room, looking through the bars of the window and into the gloom.

Outside the dappled sunlight shone through the canopies of leaves, forming an intricate mosaic patterns upon the grey stone and moist earth.

Above the soft rustling he could hear the roar of the sea beyond, the shrill cackle of a bird screaming overhead.

Misty vapour drifted amongst the trees like ghosts in a graveyard, wrapping damp tendrils about everything they touched.

Images of weeping wraiths were called to mind as James watched them inch towards the heavens, spirits unable to escape.

"An angel abashed...seeing how awful human 'goodness' really is..."

He doubted the others would be too unhappy if he wasted himself into nothing but his thoughts moved to Marianne and that alone made life worth preserving. And his pride would not allow him to abandon himself to the earth, not matter how much this capricious and often brutal administration and life wore at him.

The knife was safely stowed back in his drawer but a strange coppery stain tainted the point of its blade as if the red now scrawled on that cursed drawing had stained the silver.

Are you sure that is yours?

No. Now he thought of it he couldn't be sure, no one could be sure of anything here.

Time had passed and yet time had stood still. Whilst the sea moved and heaved the island seemed trapped in a loop. At least James felt it was.

However much he tried to recall the days that had gone by or how long he had indeed been there it was impossible.

He stood for what seemed like hours as he listened to the harsh discordant mixture of sounds that rolled in from outside. It was only when his stomach decided to join in that he moved, even if he didn't exactly feel like it, he couldn't cope with the annoying grumbling.

He put up with enough of that from others.

A rush of cold ran through him as a blast of air came from behind, he looked over his shoulder to watch a crease in his bedcovers straighten as though someone was pulling to tuck a person in. Except the room was empty.

He rubbed his eyes with his knuckles, sending stinging pain through the sensitive orbs but he could not deny what they had seen, or the chill that had not come from the flimsy window.

He continued to watch in frozen disbelief as the drawer opened, invisible papers rustled and the scratch of unseen items moved on top of the cabinet. Patterns appeared in the light sheen of dust that covered the surface as they were adjusted by equally unseen hands.

Mustering his courage James shakily edged towards the disturbance, sitting down on his bed lest his legs lose the ability to function. His eyes remained on the cabinet as the drawer slid shut with a soft click.

A bead of sweat trickled from his forehead and down his cheek, leaving a shimmering trail in its wake. His hand met nothing when he reached out to brush the air about the piece, not that he expected to find any resistance.

There was just cold air and a soft sound of starched fabric as it moved on a body.

"There is something wrong with this place," James whispered aloud, his voice echoing in the emptiness, tracing a circle over the newly polished surface.

"And what might that be?"

James jolted at the sudden voice from the doorway, turning to watch the dark form of Morbridge sidle in, unconcerned about invading his privacy, moving toward him like a tiger eying its prey. A smirk was fixed on the thin lips as he spoke in his guttural baritone.

"I must say your behaviour is more than suggesting you belong here in a different capacity," he commented frankly. "Your face has not got the look of insanity but I am well versed enough to know that is not always the case. However, I want to believe that your eyes are the cause." He glided forward. "I am always keen to sharpen my surgical triumphs; the dead offer a good look but the mind must be approached differently, you must carve that whilst it is still functioning."

His gaze was met with a defiant scowl as James stood up. He folded his arms, approaching staunchly to face the doctor directly, trying to hide the disgust that the lack of humanity caused.

"There is nothing wrong with my mind, *Sir*," he answered coldly, his voice as dark as the shadows that fell about them "I would actually question your own!"

Morbridge gave a snort, rolling his eyes. Unimpressed and unoffended.

James took a step closer and met the malicious eyes, his own visible one as cold as the ice which froze the boughs beyond the windowsill.

"And if you feel that way then kill me," he stated in the hiss of an angered serpent. "Wipe me from this hell and me into one anew, wandering aimlessly until my soul finds sanctuary."

Morbridge grinned, his teeth bright in the dark and appearing as sharp as the scalpels he used in his work.

"Far too easy. Living you are the prime example of mental decay, alas Nathaniel failed to pique you, his mind overloaded," he opened his hands in a gesture of dismissive defeat. "He is a strange one though. He does like a certain type and I suppose you did not fit his bill, maybe as well? The man didn't hold back when showing his skills."

James balled his fist, the urge to strike the man before him overwhelming, he steeled himself, moving his hand to toy with his cuff and resist the temptation.

"Well, if that is the case, Sir, that you are the face of normality," he practically spat the words "then I would rather be insane! It is your own insanity that fools you into believing that others are so afflicted!"

"The mind is a master of illusion," Morbridge said emphatically "or *delusions,* since that is what my poor children suffer."

"Suffer the children, and not for a righteous purpose," James snorted, his words caustic and cutting, he wanted to leave, tired of the immovable ideas of the other but the man's intent gaze forbade any move forth.

"A man who is mad seldom knows he is mad."

The statement broke James's trance. He strode past, his elbow connecting sharply with the doctor's own but the sharp intact of breath came from himself, pain throbbing through the joint.

"Imaginary pain? Curious," Morbridge rolled his head to watch his departure with the same fixed smile that seemed stapled to his lined face. "I must add that to my list."

"Your imaginary list gets longer then," James retorted, his voice almost drowned out by the sound of his own feet in the corridor. "Perhaps you ought to start one for yourself? It would be tangible at least."

Slowly Morbridge came forward, reaching him with ease and delving into the others pocket and a small vial was pulled out and swayed before him. A rich voice not belonging to the demented doctor swept about them.

"The dose needs reducing."

James stared at him before retreating, breaking into a fierce run.

Unblinking eyes watched him leave, frozen until the last visage of his shadow had vanished and the footfalls faded.

His voice flat and lifeless as he spoke.

"Just trust us and be silent."

Unlike James's his words did not echo, just as though they had never been spoken at all. His body seemed to stiffen, frozen in place.

"...crazy, leave him there! Not worth our time, we're done."

Chapter Twenty-Three

'You're on record, warden!'

Nathaniel's words continued to ruminate through James's head and try as he might he knew he would not be able to even approach normality if he didn't investigate.

The records of patients, past and present, were locked away in a spacious area beyond the staff rooms. Dust coated cases and cabinet held copious papers that never saw the light of day, wasting away like the person they had been kept for had done.

No light entered except from through the slit in the door and the air was colder, mustier and felt as if one was walking through cobwebs.

James hated that sensation, feeling as though sticky traps were clinging to his skin. It was impossible not to brush as oneself, trying to rid it of what wasn't there.

Thankfully there were no invisible spiders to go with them, only the real ones that occasionally scuttled from their hiding places and over to another, paying no mind to the humans that disturbed them.

His eyes took some time to adjust to the gloom as he scanned the filthy shelves for the barely visible letters, hoping that they were just tired and not disorganised. If they were out of order then any search would be impossible, he hadn't got days to trawl through them all.

His finger became almost black as he ran it over the dusty spines as he moved through them, the grime inches thick on the older files.

D, E, F...G

Swallowing hard James fought back the urge to turn back and walk away, leaving his curiosity unsatisfied. A part of him felt doing so would be safer than perhaps discovering something he would not be able to forget.

His hand reached out to pull each file out and view the name, slowing as he got closer to what he wanted.

His heart jolted and his blood ran cold as slipped out what seemed to be the thousandth file.

Grey, A...

And next to it was another; *Grey, J.*

He shoved them back with vehemence, a clammy sweat coating his palms. He didn't wish to see anymore.

• • •

Silas was idly tracing circles on a scrap of paper with a blunt pencil. Round and round until he wore the thin material down to break through to the desk beneath. Digging deeper into the wood and dulling the pencil even more, a lugubrious expression on his face.

At the sound of the keys jangling in the lock his eyes lifted, watching the door with disinterested intensity.

"Can't keep away, can you?" Silas said quietly as he sat back, a glimmer of humour appearing in his rather glazed eyes. "If you wish to swap I would gladly do so!"

James chuckled, a forced and choked sound, trailing off with a long sigh.

"I would rather not, thank you," he moved and sat heavily on the disorderly bed, massaging his forehead. "Truly Silas I fear the burden of this place will bring me down as well. Nothing here seems to be of sound mind, there is nothing I can rely on, not even myself at present."

Silas rocked on his chair, back and forth, back and forth, like a pendulum in an ever-ticking clock. He hummed to himself as he considered how best to respond, a knowledge unspoken glimmered in his luminous eyes.

"Death, in all his cowled glory, is the only thing one can truly rely on," he said philosophically, "but one should not seek him, unless he is due then he remains hidden."

James groaned, shifting to rest his head on the damp, dappled wall.

"I don't seek him. But I often think I feel him in this place, or his many aides," he looked over, condensation flattening his fringe from his eyes. "I'm a logical man, Silas, I have reluctantly accepted that perhaps things are not as straightforward as I would like and maybe there is more than meets the eye but what I sense is beyond me and I stress when I can't see any answers!"

"Seek the key," Silas said simply, leaning over to pluck something from underneath his desk. Holding open his hand to show a makeshift mould made of soap, the centre sparkling as though a key was truly forming in the fatty bar. "It is there."

"Perhaps but I..."

James's words trailed off as he heard the soft footsteps outside and the rustle of a starched fabric as the unseen form walked.

His eyes were wide as he looked over, hissing under his breath. "Do you hear that?"

"Indeed. Perhaps. Maybe?" Silas chuckled and slipped lower in his chair, his hands toying with the soap as they rested on his stomach. "One hears so many discordant sounds in the workaday world!"

He laughed in an oddly musical fashion, tossing the mould into the corner where it was swallowed by the shadows that permanently resided there, untouched by the sun.

"Just be assured it is not likely to be such a frightful occurrence like the drummer of Cortachy!"

"Heaven forbid," James muttered without really registering the words, and should he have it was doubtful that the implications would have been understood. "Just don't think you are accompanying me, it would be more than my life is worth."

"Wouldn't even consider it, my dear friend!" Silas tossed his hair back which fell in silver wave about his slender person. "I remain here as always and say nothing of what passes betwixt us!"

James cast an incredulous gaze towards him before pausing at the door, the sounds so clear it was almost as though it was wide open and not sealed like the prison it pretended not to be. And yet the corridor, at first glance, seemed deserted.

The air seemed hazy, flickering like static, coupled by a soft hiss that joined the other odd sounds.

He paused as Marianne's voice filled his ears, dulling the noises and taking his mind from the strangeness of the atmosphere.

'Lights so soft, they dance like stars,
Are we closer to the other side?
Can I wish this world away,
And escape the shadows from which I hide?'

The words echoed mournfully about him as he edged down the gauzy passage, every step feeling slow and heavy.

'Like walking in a dream,' he mused to himself as he felt for the unusually comforting cold of the wall, 'but I cannot wake from this.'

A blurred white form rushed past him, rustling as it went, the soft click of flat heels echoing in its wake.

James narrowed his eyes, trying to bring the figure into focus before it swung around the corner but the edges were too indistinct, impossible to glean anymore detail. Only that it was a humanoid form, one he felt was female.

'James?'

The voice came from all directions, flowing about him like a gentle river, clinging to him like droplets of rain.

"Keep moving," he ordered himself in a hushed, panicked voice, wringing his hands nervously as he pushed himself on. "This has to be solved."

His heart almost burst from his chest as the doors of the rooms flew open with a crescendo of bangs, one after the other. The sound taking some time to stop echoing both in the passage and in his ears. He felt cold, as though ice had taken the place of the blood in his veins, slowly freezing him.

Swallowing hard he looked into one of the gaping rooms,

expecting the chained individual to be wrenching at the bounds to escape their physical agony if not the emotional.

But it was empty. They were all empty.

Cold stone met his eyes, the mists forming human forms, wandering to and fro, passing through walls to somewhere invisible to his sight.

A flash of blue caused him to turn, feeling the air move as it moved by leaving a scent of clinical perfume.

When it past another figure, crystal clear, stood there. Her clothes had changed, no longer the short dress but garbed in a longer black one, floating under her knees, the hem wispy and unfocused. The only part of her that was and made him sense she was not of this world.

She was looking towards him, *through* him, towards Silas's room, her eyes sparkling with unshed tears, the trails of those that had fallen evident on the rouged cheeks, stark against the creamy skin.

'I keep my faith? What more can I do? Demons never win, or they cannot be allowed to.'

She seemed to pause as though listening to someone responding, even though nothing stirred behind him, everything seemed to still. White noise hissing in his ears like the waves against a rocky shore.

Shifting uncomfortably, she wrung her slender hands, the movement making her flicker.

'...surround with happy memories? A hard ask, death seemed the only viable option, a full proof solution for peace and away from the shadows.'

A long sigh emanated from her, a soft wind beginning to blow and slowly, like the fragile clouds, wisps of her flowed away with it.

Her hand drifted to her side, something falling softly to the floor as she faded, landing with a rustle.

Summoning the courage lying flat in his stomach James moved toward the fallen object, seeing as he drew closer that it was a balled-up paper.

He fingered it gingerly, feeling the sharp edges to ascertain its corporeality, he'd been tricked all too often by lack of substance to risk anymore.

He unfolded it heedlessly, not caring should the flimsy material tear, it was already crumpled and frayed.

When the faded edge of the childish drawing appeared, he clenched his fist, crushing it even more before hurling it into the shadows, swearing wickedly under his breath.

The breath was pulled from his lungs as a rush of air whipped past him, pulling the balled-up paper from its resting place and sending it bouncing down the stairs, disappearing into the darkness. James let out a sigh of frustration and followed after it, the haziness feeling thinner now the figures had dissipated and although the air still felt peculiar it no longer felt as though he was traipsing through quick sand.

Despite the subconscious bickering between sense and the unease of his nerves James made his way carefully down the bleak stairway. No sound vibrated upward toward him, no subtle shuffle of a human moving from his uncomfortable position.

The stairwell seemed longer, twisting further down into the unseen, winding and wild. When he thought about it, he hadn't even known the stairs were this close to where he had been. But a building was stagnant, he knew better than to think it moved.

All he could think of at that moment was retrieving the picture lest the wrong hands find it and cast even more doubt upon him. Knowing he was of sound mind was little consolation, since he knew no one else besides Marianne and Silas would back him.

And who would take the word of those locked away as genuine? He even questioned himself for allowing them to become more than simple faces in a room, just part of a monotonous job.

'One I don't even remember being without,' James mused as he made his way down yet another flight of stone steps 'a pure flight of fancy since life has not revolved about this damned place.'

He didn't remember reaching the basement. Not until his foot landed on flat stone.

Chapter Twenty-Four

The air seemed closer than ever as James reached the base of the ever-winding stairs that had felt like they had twisted and turned to the span the abyss. Common sense told him that it couldn't have been any longer than before, that it was just his tired imagination making everything more difficult.

"How in God's name did it fall this far?" he asked aloud, his voice echoing in the emptiness as his eyes became used to the richer gloom. "No breeze should have been able to send it much beyond the first few stairs. And if it had then it should be resting here."

There was no one else down here. None of the others came this way unless they had no other choice, they avoided it like the plague, so there was not even an iota of a chance that someone had picked up the crumpled picture.

Despite the trepidation churning in his guts he continued forward, the silence unbearable, even his footsteps seemed to be swallowed by the shadows.

The secure doors swung on their hinges, swaying in an unfelt draught, dust drifting lethargically from settled sheets on the handles and floor as though no one had trod there for some time.

It tickled his nostrils as he moved further, wafting it from his vision, his eyes focused on the rooms to his sides unable to blink. Only one was of interest and his chest tightened the near he got to the swinging door.

He expected to hear the soft and sinister sounds of the chains as the male shifted, the low growling laughter as he sensed the presence and that tormenting voice.

But only silence reigned.

A small crackle sounded like breaking glass in the quiet and he watched in amazement as the crumpled ball rolled from the corner and into the dreaded room, unfurling as it went as though it was beckoning him to follow.

James darted forward in an attempt to seize it before it passed over the threshold but it slipped away from his outstretched fingers, rolling into the corner where chain hung limply, the thick jacket of dust signifying they had been without an occupant for many months.

No sign of Nathaniel remained.

James's body moved in slow motion as he leant forward to pick up the errant paper, surveying the empty area, the sense of foreboding so strong that he felt it would crush him. His hand closed on the paper, allowing it to slowly open.

Sickness washed over him as the image revealed itself. That once happy picture was now a bloodbath.

The figures were all there again but no longer a smiling family. The adults lay prone on the floor, scribbled red pooled beneath them, their mouths twisted into grimaces, eyes drawn in grey, glassy and lost to the world.

The female girl stood near, her dress torn and bloody gashes etched into her thighs, lips open in a silent scream, her hands spiked and clutching her face.

The boy. The boy sat wide eyed, his expression vacant as he looked at the carnage before him, a knife, the hilt identical to the one that lay in James's draw, lay haphazardly nearby. His wrist was malformed, twisted and broken.

James's eyes were irresistibly drawn to his own left wrist, his eyes widening at the sight of white scar tissue, heaving and pulsating as though gasping for breath.

The picture fluttered to the floor as his fingers lost their grip, nausea heaving in his stomach as the paper convulsed, the red ink pooling from the image, a slow ooze swallowing it as the ghastly scarlet shroud covered the floor.

A cacophony of voices rang through his ears, men, women, and children, their words echoing and merging together into a violent symphony.

'This isn't the right way...'

'Shut your mouth or I'll shut it for you!'

'Don't leave me, James!'

James clamped his hands over his ears, closing his eyes tightly but the sound seemed present in his head, a roll of thunder broke through the haunted images and screaming voices in his head, the howl of wind audible as it wailed above.

The massive metal doors swung back, wrenched by an unseen force, and crashed against the wall that held them, sending a spray of chipped stone to the ground. The cloud billowed over, forcing into his lungs as he breathed, causing him to give in to a painful cough that wracked his body. Phlegm and blood intermingled in his throat as his body tried to force out the dirt that attempted to choke him.

"Damn it!" He spat a congealed lump onto the floor where it slid down into a crack leaving a trail of salvia behind.

Wiping the residue away with his sleeve James turned and headed the way he had come, searching for the stairs to lead him from the tenth circle.

The corridor seemed to stretch out, like the spiral of the inferno it twisted and distorted, blurred and cleared.

His feet stumbled on the heaving concrete, bulging and sinking as though the earth beneath was stirring. His body twisted as he collided with the wall and fell painfully to his knees, the fabric of his trousers tearing as it chafed on the stone. Blood trickled from the minor scrape, staining the fabric.

The warmth, followed by the sticky coolness as the fluid thickened, brought him back to his senses and with effort he pulled himself to his feet.

Voices followed like lost souls. Whispering, pleading and cursing. Voices he knew, voices he *thought* he knew.

"Stop this!" His own tone rang loud to break through the rabble. "I will not be a pawn in your game!"

He retreated doggedly, determined to locate the stairs that eluded him. It seemed like he was walking for miles through identical scenery, running on a repetitive reel. Each time he rounded a corner, hoping to see the dusty steps he was disappointed, seeing only the sterile surroundings begin again.

He froze as a dark form glided towards him, the outline of the doctor drew closer, so close he could see the sweat beads pool on the frowning forehead, glittering almost as much as the long needle held in his hand.

It lifted, a droplet of clear fluid clinging to the point, shaking violently as the form flickered and fading.

James didn't want to see the result of this projection, lurching through the figure as though it wasn't even there, just another ghost of his imagination.

He was about to give up when, finally, his eyes alighted on a soft light pouring from the upper levels illuminating the dirty stairway. Never had he been so glad to see a way to the rooms above.

"Thank the Gods," he muttered in breathless relief, his body drooping as the tension drained from his muscles and he mounted the stairs.

His legs began to feel tired as the climb seemed, like the corridors, to stretch out beyond logical reason.

'James?'

Looking up James saw the lovely figure of Marianne smiling tenderly at him at the top of the steps, a vision of loveliness in the dark, opening her arms to him.

'A touch can take away the pain,' she said softly, her smile never wavering as her voice filled his mind. *'You told me that once before I went away.'*

"I did?" James cupped her face, his thumbs lifting her head to gaze into her soulful eyes "I knew you?"

'You know much, but perhaps not as much as you once did.'

James shook his head slowly in bewilderment, he could not respond as there was nothing to say. Everyone in this place seemed to talk in riddles and they went over his head. Instead he drew her to him, holding her close and breathing in her scent, wondering how she had been before the asylum had wasted the flesh from her bones.

A strange sensation overtook him as he held her. Her body felt as though it throbbed, the bones beginning to feel less prominent, her chest receding to flatten against her.

The surroundings suddenly seemed taller, wider.

He pulled back to view her at arm's length, suppressing a cry of alarm as a child looked back at him.

The limpid eyes that occupied the rounder face made it clear that it was still Marianne who stood before him.

Slowly he backed away, looking down at his own hands, hands of a young boy, small and smooth.

'Do you know me now?'

"I..." The voice that left his choked throat was unbroken. A choir boy's lilting tone.

He lifted his gaze from her, looking over the rounded shoulder to see the ghostly woman in the near distance, her hand reaching towards him, beckoning.

And then there was white.

Chapter Twenty-Five

One...

'James? Please come back to me!'

Two...

'Cut his throat! That'll shut him up!'

Three...

'This isn't right.'

All the way to ten.

When James's vision finally returned, a slow process with colours leaking through blankness like oil through a canvas, slowly forming blurred images that gradually cleared, he was stood back in the corridor leading to the staff rooms.

The lack of sound, except for the wind shaking the windows, shouldn't have been as jarring as it was. If all was run as standard then the staff were performing their assigned duties and were randomly placed around the building.

But, as James knew all too well, that seldom happened and always a handful, if not all, of the other warders were wasting their time talking or doing nothing.

"For the love of God, I have to stop thinking the worst!" James rebuked himself, flinching as he heard his voice in the quiet, adding rather diffidently, "And I have to stop talking aloud to myself."

Through the crack in the door he could make out figures sat around the table, steam trailing from cups placed near their elbows. He squinted as he approached, trying to work out why they were so still, why no sound came from within but he could see nothing except the dull interior he was used to.

The door banged against the wall as he shoved it open as though it weighed as much as a leaf in autumn.

James stared at the scene that met him, his hand frozen on the door panel. It was like gazing on an unpleasant landscape on an unknown artist.

Several staff members stood frozen in time, still as statues as they sat or stood dotted about the room. Not a hair twitched, nor did their shadows waiver as the light shifted. It was though they were holograms or remnants of a time long ago.

James moved about them in listless wonder, pausing by the male who had caught his hand in the door, waving the self-same one before the vacant eyes but received no response. He stared ahead as though the orbs were made of glass like the stag's heads that sometimes decorated the walls of inns.

As he traversed the figures, examining them silently, coldness fell over the room. The walls began to shake, cracks opening in them like in infected sores.

From outside the trees moaned as their branches stretched painfully, the briars that embraced them following suit. As if they were snakes, covered in venomous barbs, they slithered from the openings, their thorns clattering on the floor, cracking about the limbs of the furniture and climbing the walls.

Outside a deafening roar of thunder shook the building, the room illuminated in a sheet of blue that took his sight and skewed his vision.

James's hand flew up to cover his eyes, waiting for the needles of pain that pierced his head to subside, listening to the threatening noises of nature continue.

When the brightness faded and his vision returned the room was empty. It was as though nothing had ever been there. No cracks, no vines.

"Just an empty room..."

His heart began to palpitate madly as he tried to keep his cool, searching his convoluted mind for some sense of logic. But there was none, the only explanation was a trick of the mind but one so vivid even that seemed implausible.

"Unless I really am losing my sanity," James muttered in a hissed whisper, listening to every echoed syllable as if the stains of madness would be audible. But his voice was as always, albeit louder in the quiet.

All comprehension of time and all his senses seemed to fade as his mind became clouded, delving deeper into all the crevices that he could reach, far shallower than he would have liked.

A sharp smell of burning broke the spell he had cast upon himself, piercing his nostrils and painting his throat.

Wisps of grey smoke were seeping underneath the doorway and through the keyhole, carrying with it a deathly silence. No sound of timber crackling as flames ate into it or cries of terror from enclosed inmates echoed.

To some that might have settled them, that perhaps it was controlled, but to James it simply made the situation even more unsettling. Even when Morbridge burnt the deceased in the grounds there was still some noise, even if the life was only from the blaze.

He couldn't ignore it though; his own life could depend on it if there was a fire somewhere. And also Marianne and Silas, all the lives here mattered. Even Morbridge, even if he resented thinking it.

"If this is nothing then I don't know what to do," James headed towards the smell, pushing the door open forcefully in his frustration, "except admit that my mind is lost to the darkness in this place."

The stench heightened the further he went as if the very walls themselves were pulsing it from within the stone. The smoke was becoming thicker, beginning to resemble the gauzy mists that hovered about the damp earth outside when heat managed to get through.

As he passed through the vestibule the fog from beyond joined the smoke, the doors ajar and allowing the air to kindle the hidden flames further and chase the heat that was sure to come.

The doors of the cells hung open, swaying on breaking hinges coated in coppery rust that hadn't been there before. The rooms behind were hazy, even without the smoke, and seemed to be set between worlds.

James's brow wrinkled in confusion but he disregarded it for the time as pulled himself away from the first door.

His heart nearly flew from his chest as the door slammed shut with a cavernous crash, the others following one by one in a deafening performance that echoed on in his head and throughout the building, the floors seeming to pulse with the ferocity of the noise.

James clasped his hands over his pained ears in an effort to drown it out while it subsided, it barely dulled it, the clang resounding for what seemed like an eternity, morphing into a low ring before it ceased and left him feeling as though his bones trembled beneath his skin.

Taking a moment to calm himself he looked forward through the ever thickening smoke into a dismal beyond. Shapes seemed to form, humanoid and featureless, morphing and curling with the greyness.

'I have to go on,' he thought more stolidly than he felt as he fixed his concentration on the two faces he held dear, made easier as the singing voice of Marianne filled his head, chanting a verse in languid tone.

'Sunlight chases darkness
But the shadows still remain.
Reaching through the crevices
To choke all hearts insane.

The sadness reeks eternally
And the reaper reaps his toll
The pyres ever smoulder
At the whim of those who claim control.'

He quickened his pace.

Chapter Twenty-Six

The heat became stifling the further James moved, seeming to come from the centre of the building, rising as though from the pits of Hell themselves.

The air was thick and choked his straining lungs which frantically throbbed in search for oxygen.

He refused to allow that to slow him. If anything it pushed him forward more quickly, his mind fixed only on those he wanted to take from this place, to save from the lingering death and decay. However that might come.

He forced onward, through the oppressive climate, through each identical corridor that seemed even longer than before, stretching like an endless serpent, but finally relief flood his tense tendons as his eyes alighted on one door that remained shut.

'It makes sense,' he thought as he made his way towards it, leaning his weight on the walls as his body struggled to filter air through to him, 'that if Silas remains the door would be shut.'

Sense or logic seemed to have no power though and the closer he edged the more he began to doubt himself, his hands trembled badly as he reached for the handle, the metal heated and painful to grip.

Fighting the sting he wrenched the protesting door open, balking at the fury of the heat from the fire that had eaten through the softer bedding Silas was afforded.

Silas himself remained as the fire grew around him, the tongues licking about the heavy wood chair, examining his nails as though it was a normal, mundane day and showing no sign of feeling the effects of the scarlet fury.

At James's entrance he lifted his lidded eyes and rose elegantly, brushing the flaming embers from his hair as they if they were nothing but dust.

He smiled faintly as he sidled over, offering an eerily pale hand.

"Come, my friend, let us leave this accursed place."

"But Marianne," James said, taking hold of the proffered hand "we can't leave her here, she'll…"

Silas placed his free hand lightly on James's cheek, hushing him with a soothing gaze and the continuous, idle smile.

"Fear not, she will meet us, there are ways to break any chain and we have finally weakened ours. Now you just need to release your own."

The window behind gave a scream, the glass shattering into brilliant shards that littered the floor to reflect the growing flames that were consuming the desk.

Silas nudged James through the doorway with his elbow, following a few steps behind as though on a morning stroll.

As the door swung shut on its own accord James scanned the corridor in search of the clearest route to take, the smoke confusing his sense of direction and filling his head and sinuses, making it hard to remember anything.

His eyes fell on a figure half hidden in the grey and immediately recognised the shape and form of Marianne, her features becoming clearer as she glided with ghostly grace towards them, that esoteric smile still on her lips.

"The island is falling. It began to crack some time ago, when figures that were never here began to walk; now it is failing and how beautiful it shall be!"

She clasped her hands together in an excitable silent prayer, her eyes sparkling intensely in the gloom. Silas smiled and stepped forward, each step he took cracking the floor as though it were the most fragile glass. The splintering sound hurt his head, thumping in his skull as if that too was breaking.

Marianne saw the flinch and held out her hand, clasping his fingertips to draw him to her, guide him across the unstable flooring. He kept her gaze, focused on those knowing eyes that dispelled his fears with the glow of friendship and compassion.

He didn't feel the sensation of walking, lost in those eyes and unaware of anything except the occasional tickle from the silvery locks of hair as Silas walked near him, wafting by the fiery air. Every sound about him paled into nothing; the crackles, the echoes, nothing reached his ears for some time.

When it did it was a frantic hiss of confused voices and sentences that made little sense and yet he knew he'd heard them all before.

'James...Behold the titanium ghost...Where are we going...This isn't the right way!'

Louder and louder they filled his head, a trickling rivulet turned into a furious cascade, the sound of his own cry of pain barely rose above them.

Faces flashed before his eyes, those he knew and those he thought he knew.

White stars covered Marianne's face and his legs crumpled beneath him, his hands releasing hers to clamp over his ears. He didn't feel the floor as he fell, just emptiness and soothing, cradling darkness.

The next thing he felt was the soft feel of mizzle clinging to his skin, a combination of weeping rain and spray from the violent sea that rocked the island, making it moan as it tore at the rocky tendons. A warm hand covered his right cheek as Marianne leant over him, urging him silently to get up.

"We cannot dally here," Silas said quietly as he stood nearby, concern in his brilliant green eyes. "This is your chance and you must seize it. Otherwise we begin again."

"Wh-what do you mean?" James drawled, his tongue feeling slack in his mouth as he rolled his head over weakly "what do you mean that we'd begin again? You make no sense, *nothing* makes sense!"

Leaning down Silas took his hands, urging him to his feet. They were outside, the sea visible, thrashing against the corroding cliffs. He watched in awed silence as the thick greenery that had shielded their view for so long fell into the vortex of water, consumed by ravenous waves.

145

Bones of former patients that had been discarded beneath the verdure crumbled as they were unearthed by the heave of the earth, the skulls grinning mockingly towards the trio before they too fell away.

"You don't belong here, James, you never did," Silas said calmly, looking to Marianne who nodded in agreement. "Look in your hand."

James tentatively opened his fingers which he had not realised until then had been clenched, a sticky substance clung to them but he barely felt it, staring in wonder at the silver key lying in his palm.

"It was yours to craft and unless you use it then all will be lost."

He swept his arm towards the distance. Tiny lights, like thousands of fireflies, were stirring from the earth and the churning waters. They rose slowly, coming together as if forming an intricate jigsaw, creating a shimmering bridge to stretch across the sea and to the vast beyond.

"You must go. Before the islands falls and history repeats itself."

James looked over his shoulder at the smouldering grey walls as the flames weaves higher towards the glow of the pagan moon. Stagnant silence came from within, if any were still held captive in the blackening stone they felt no pain as fire peeled the skin from the flesh.

He felt Silas take hold of his upper arm and turned to meet the languid eyes.

"I-I can't," James looked from him to Marianne "I cannot leave you, you will perish!"

"Perhaps, perhaps not," came the patient answer, spindly fingers sliding down his limb to take his hand, "but trust me as your friend when I say it is for the best. Neither man nor beast should be ensnared in such a prison."

As he spoke James felt his hand burn as the key began to glow, his uniform fraying at the seams and the colour bleeding away from it, melting into the mud beneath his feet.

He took an unsteady step towards the translucent structure before glancing back to them, his heart aching with anxiety and a sense of loss.

"Will I see you again? Either of you?"

"It is not for me to predict," Silas smiled cryptically. "Life, much like the mind, is a strange thing. Truly I would go anywhere with you, we both would, but it would cause more havoc."

His hair wafted around him, concealing his features like a sheer veil, he shook his head to fend it back, the glow from behind him making him seem transparent.

Marianne stood a few paces behind, her eyes smiled but she sent no words, merely bowing her head gently in James's direction.

"All will become lucid once you have found your way."

James held back from replying that he doubted anything would make any sense. His entire life, of which he remembered, seemed to have been blighted by confusion.

Silas sensed the words but he didn't say anything, looking away to dust the embers from his person which glowed like fireflies as they clung to him.

Their eyes held for some moments before James's head dropped resignedly. Slowly he took a step towards the glowing bridge, seeing lights dancing in the distance.

Below the structure the sea still raged but no sound came from it, something that made the situation more terrifying and foreboding. But those lights, so white, so bright, they beckoned, warm and peaceful as if they were the lure to the gates of paradise.

With one final look towards Marianne and Silas he began forwards, the bridge fading away behind him.

The pair turned in tandem, walking away towards the burning asylum, the flames reddening the dead air about them.

Chapter Twenty-Seven

"Will you get that?" Anneliese looked up from staring at the soft glow of the screen as the bell broke her concentration and the heavy tones from the radio. "I'm trying to finish my homework."

"Never bothered you before," her younger brother grumbled, tossing his comic onto the well frayed cushion as he rolled himself onto the floor. "Bet you're looking at porn."

"I am not; you're the one who probably does that, *if* you even know what it is!" The bell sounded again, longer this time, followed by a sharp knocking. "Just get it, will you? Maybe mom and dad forget their keys, you know how wound up he gets about these benefit things."

"Fine," James got to his feet and slouched towards the door, pausing in the hallway. "And why would look at that stuff? Girls are gross. And you can't be working either, listening to that."

"If people can work listening to the Spice Girls then I can work listening to Titanium Ghost."

"You only listen because you fancy the lead singer," James retorted loudly as he wandered into the gloom of the hallway.

Anneliese frowned and leant around to call after him.

"The fact he's hot is just a bonus, besides I can only drool can't I? Dante doesn't like girls," she looked at the cover photo of the album with a girlish grin, hearing the click as the catch was lifted.

"Aren't a lot of his fans girls?"

"Never mind."

Anneliese sat back in the chair, clicking the spellcheck of the document she was working on, ignoring the muffled talk from outside, assuming it was one of the neighbours coming to check on them. At fourteen it was irritating to think their parents still needed to employ Big Brother to keep an eye of things.

"Anneliese?" She looked up to see James had returned, looking puzzled as he stood in the doorway fidgeting "can you come here?"

"What is it? Charity hawker?"

"Police."

The smile abruptly faded from her lips and she slammed the laptop shut to hurry to the open door, the air freezing as it blew in.

Two men in dark clothing stood there looking somewhat impatient, the one tapping his foot sharply against the stone step.

As she emerged the sharp-eyed man to the right flashed a badge, too swiftly for her to see it properly in the gloom.

"Miss Grey? You're Stephen and Gemma's daughter, correct?" His voice was cutting and had a cold, clinical edge to it, his impenetrable eyes and inscrutable countenance giving little away.

"Y-yes, Sir," Anneliese stammered, her eyes flitting from one to the other. "Do-do you want to come in?"

"No." The answer was terse. "You need to come with us, both of you."

Anneliese frowned, edging neared to her brother protectively. Despite the official look to the badge, what she had been able to catch sight of, something seemed odd. Yet maybe she was being paranoid.

She swallowed, looking up as confidently as she could in an attempt to portray the composed adult she tried to be.

"Could you at least tell me what this is about? Our parents aren't here and I'd be an idiot to drag my brother out without knowing, even if you are police."

"We know your parents aren't here," the second man spoke up, dark blond hair framing his face. "That's why we've come; there's been a...incident. Nothing serious, just a robbery, sad to say that's a risk when you're a success in the banking world. We just need you to come back to the station, they haven't been able to contact anyone and they don't want you alone."

Anneliese paled, her rosy cheeks fading to ashen ivory as she nodded, feeling James cling to her arm as he tried to process the words also. She moved her hand to stroke his hair, brushing it away from the mismatched eyes before patting his shoulder encouragingly.

"Go fetch your coat, James, and mine," she caught hold of him as he turned to obey, smiling comfortingly. "Don't worry, it'll be OK."

The latter words seemed to be a muttered prayer to convince herself more than him.

"Of course it will," the older man said tersely. "You'll be back before you know it."

Only James noticed the mysterious smile that passed between the pair as he reached towards the coat rack. Slowly he took the both thick jackets from the pegs, fastening the buttons of his own as he rejoined his sister, his feet feeling heavy as though his shoes were lined with weights and trying to restrain him.

"Sweet, let's go."

The winter wind sliced neatly through them like razor blades as they stepped from the warmth of the house and into the night.

"Why isn't your car marked?" James asked as he shut the door and looked to where a black hatchback was parked askew on the kerbside.

"Because there was no emergency and it would just cause alarm to have a fully equip car draw up, wouldn't it?"

In the children's mind the answer made sense.

The first man opened the door, letting out the scent of stale smoke which had been clinging to the leather upholstery.

"Better than the smell of a damp dog," he commented with a dismissive shrug. "Even worse if they piss in the back."

Anneliese chuckled nervously at the words and clambered in, sliding across to make room for James beside her. The empty cigarette packet stuffed between the chairs didn't strike her as something police would have but maybe it was just from a previous occupant and they hadn't noticed.

"Get in the middle," the man ordered James. "You'll need someone in the back with you."

"OK."

James's voice was not above a whisper as he shuffled to his sister; even the lightest of breezes would have masked it. He sat tensely beside her, entwining his fingers with her own.

The sound of the doors locking jarred him and his muscles contracted even more, sounding so loud in the silence of the night.

Nothing stirred as the engine purred into life, the only movement the shaking of Anneliese's hand as they set off down the street, the roads seeming luminous from the bright lights of the lamps and glow from peaceful houses reflecting from the residue of recent rain.

It was a good ten minutes before the silence was broken. Anneliese's voice was shaky and tinged with fear as she looked away from the window.

"Sir, this isn't the right way, I know where the station is."

There was no answer.

They had turned left at the main island and headed down into the backstreets, the places were illicit drug deals took place and alcoholics loitered after hours. There were hardly any lights since they had been smashed long ago and even the police didn't like patrolling there.

Abandoned building loomed above, grey and sombre and blocking the moon and the smattering of stars in the inky sky.

"Let us out…"

"Shut your mouth or I'll cut it from ear to ear!" The flash of a blade reflected in the blond man's eyes as he withdrew it from the concealed pocket, pointing it toward her threateningly.

"But where are you taking us?"

"Shut it!"

The tip of the knife touched James's neck and instantly Anneliese snapped her lips shut to form a thin line, her jaw tensed.

James looked at her helplessly, knowing she was feeling as hopeless and terrified as he was as the car continued towards the bleak industrial estate, the buildings empty and falling apart. The headlights reflected off shards of glass from smashed windows, illuminating crude graffiti sprayed on the stone.

The tyres squealed to a halt outside one of the dingy structures, the iron that had once covered the door rusted and hanging loose.

The man driving turned to look at them, his expression concealed by the shadows.

"Try to run and you'll end up like your parents, both of whom you're about to see, part of them anyway, my friend here works wonder with a blade."

It had been easy enough to lure the adults away with the threat of harm to the children, to force them to hand over the money they had and the codes to the safe that was in the house. Neither had expected the pair to be there, assuming they would be staying elsewhere with other relatives, from their observations that normally occurred.

They had long ago discovered that petty crime didn't pay and left them open to an easy arrest. A slower and more methodical approach could be tedious but the reward was great. Their targets were always scouted, making certain that they were successful but widely unknown; a famous face would be lucrative but too risky.

James felt a strong grip on his collar as he was dragged from the seat. He kicked out, trying to wriggle free but instead the grip tightened, the fabric squeezing his airways and choking him into a reluctant submission.

Anneliese followed, her entire body trembling as she watched her brother being used as a pawn, a lure to get her to obey. She wouldn't leave him, even if their relationship was strained like any siblings, she was his sister and she should have protected him.

'I should've known better...'

Her thoughts were all of self blame as she proceeded into the dark of the warehouse, the clinging air thick with dust and the scent of decay.

The next few hours were a blur of pain, violation and despair.

Anneliese vomited as she saw the mutilated corpses that had once been their parents. Those arms that had embraced them on so many occasions draped over split bodied, hanging on by stretched tendons.

She couldn't even muster a scream one of the men shoved her

back onto the filthy floor, pinning her with his bodyweight as her brother watched, the offending knife shoved into his hand.

'Whose prints will it have now? It'll be easy to concoct a story of a retarded child who lost it.'

James eyes glazed over, trying to leave his body, the coldness and terror weighty enough to crush his heart.

This wasn't happening. He wasn't here, he was far away. Just a witness in a nightmarish dream who was envisioning the scene unfold. A simple turn of thought could change this.

Picture it, picture it! Go away, to an island lost in times gone by, safe at sea with these fiends locked away. He was the guard with the key.

He vaguely heard noise about him as he began to fade but they were overshadowed by the sounds of a powerful ocean.

"What the hell is wrong with him?"

Anneliese was pushed away, sobbing violently as the man looked around at James who had begun to slump, eyes wide but vacant.

"The kids just crazy; kill him, she ain't going to talk if she knows what's good for her and he isn't good for anything."

The blond glared at him and shook his head defiantly.

"No way, I don't kill children. There's a line I don't cross."

They turned and watched as James slowly sank down, falling into the waves he had created. He heard no more, not the silky voice of a stranger whose long hair brushed his cooling skin, the blaring sirens or his sisters' pleas.

Chapter Twenty-Eight

"What happened after that?"

The doctor looked up from the pile of notes on the desk to the woman sat opposite, her hands folded but jittery in her lap.

"We were found by a homeless man," Anneliese continued, a diamante tear sparkling in her eye. "I say man; they had such long hair it was impossible to tell, but they kept us occupied, talking on and on about a partner and his ambles about the cemeteries."

She gave a sorrowful sigh, her hair falling forward as her head dropped. She had been through this so often and yet it never became any easier. Sometimes it felt as though it only became worse, seeing him lying there with tubes and fluids keeping him alive.

"James wasn't there anymore, he just sank into sleep. You've seen yourself, he has moments of lucidity but much of the time he just seems lost to the world."

The doctor nodded patiently as he scanned the notes, trying to keep a neutral expression even though the descriptions were repulsive even to him.

"I read to him," she said mournfully "I don't want him to wake with the mind of a child so I've tried all sorts of books, the history ones he used to love and I've told him about those he knew, the good and the bad. Even about the friend he once had, poor girl was terribly abused but she's moved on, just like I want him to move on, like we both need to."

Seeing the man nod sparked a small hope inside her, one lone star in an otherwise eternal night.

"It may do, most experts say that the brain is still receptive even if the body isn't. It's how hypnosis is supposed to work."

"I don't understand how this happened," Anneliese gave a sigh and the tear finally fell "I went through Hell also but my reactions…"

"The mind is strange and unique to each person," the doctor answered softly, pushing a box of tissues towards her. "Clearly he felt that to escape his demons he needed to leave reality entirely. They call it a sleeping beauty syndrome, at least in layman's words, some term it parasomnia. It's a wide spectrum."

"Sometimes I think he sees me. His eyes open and he looks at me as if he's returned for a while but then he just sinks away again, almost as if he's afraid."

Anneliese took a fragile Kleenex and blew her nose, more tears soaking into it. Over the years she had cried enough to fill a well but weeping wasn't going to help anyone.

"He's been like this a long time, it will be a shock to his system when he wakes," the doctor looked thoughtful "I've even heard of cases where people have lived entirely different lives in their dreams. He'll have a lot to get used to but I'm certain it can be done and we will work with you each step of the way."

"I would say it's up to the gods," Anneliese whispered and she slowly got to her feet and reached to gather her bag, "but I can't, our fates are ours and decided by the paths we choose when they are offered. Unfortunately they cross other people's bad trails."

Her hand shook and the faux leather bag tipped over with the contents slipping from inside. She muttered crossly, leaning to push them back in.

"The Victorians?" The doctor smiled as he noticed the title of the book she carried. "Interesting topic, I suppose you learn things while you read to him as well."

"James always enjoyed history," Anneliese said as she fingered the book tenderly "I want him to enjoy what gets through to him."

Shouldering the bag she nodded her goodbye and headed towards the light of the exit, her heels clicking in tandem with the beep of many monitors.

She paused once, looking through the glass of a door at the ghostly pale figure that lay prone and unconscious, almost camouflaged against the white of the starched sheets. She pressed a hand against the coolness of the door, swallowing her sadness.

No longer was the bony form the brother who had brought such joy and annoyance to her in their younger years.

"Fight on, James," she whispered, "please wake and we will move on."

It seemed an age. Standing there listening to the hypnotic beep that never ceased, that counted the heartbeats that gave her hope.

Hope sprang eternal after all.

Lightning Source UK Ltd.
Milton Keynes UK
UKHW010633130122
397082UK00002B/280